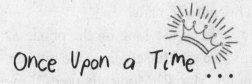

Once Upon a Time ...

This was the part Tilly Johnson loved best – when the princess casts off her shackles and flees from her faraway town to embrace who she truly is.

Spinning around in front of the small television, Matilda extended her arms and sung along with the princess about letting go. Suddenly she wasn't in her dimly-lit lounge in Dullerton anymore, but on a frozen hillside, the air whipping past her cheeks and tangling her brown curls.

She spun around and around as the snow swirled like a tornado. She was about to reach the song's crescendo when the door to the lounge flung open, revealing her sister's scowling face.

'Tilly, shut up,' Monica declared. 'Some of us are trying to have a conversation.' She yanked on the phone she'd managed to pull an impressive three feet beyond the confines of the kitchen. Its chord stretched worryingly thin as she wound it around her painted nails.

'You've been too long on the phone as it is!' another voice said tersely from the kitchen.

'Shut up, Maria!' Monica barked. 'I'm almost done.'

Then, in a considerably softer tone, she said directly in to the phone she was clutching too tightly, 'Patrick, I'm so sorry. It's my stupid sisters.'

Tilly glanced longingly at the television where her movie continued to play, but the magic had already left the lounge. She could feel the coarse carpet beneath her bare feet where there should have been the crisp sharpness of snow.

'Can I finish my movie?' She shot her sister a pitiful glance.

'No!' Monica shouted, nostrils flaring angrily. She was careful to clamp a hand down over the phone's mouthpiece so Patrick wouldn't hear her.

PAPER Princess

CARYS JONES

Published by Accent Press Ltd 2016

Paperback ISBN: 9781786150646
    ebook ISBN: 9781786151025

'Turn it off!' she instructed. 'And take off that stupid dress. You're too old to look so ridiculous.'

The door was slammed shut as Tilly looked down forlornly at her sparkling blue dress. It had been one of her favourite gifts that previous Christmas and she wore it as often as possible. What did Monica mean that she was too old? Tilly fingered the fragile fabric, admiring the way it glistened in the light. Surely she wasn't too old to dress up? Had twelve become the new twenty?

The celebration of her twelfth birthday had been unusually subdued that year but Tilly could still smell the smoke from the candles she blew out just three days ago. She held the memory of her birthday close in her mind, trying to prolong the magic that only birthdays and Christmas seem able to bring.

'Get off the phone!' she could hear her sisters arguing on the other side of the thin door. The wood shook fearfully each time they raised their voices.

'Put it down, Monica! You don't own the phone!'

The door continued to shake as something

banged against it. Tilly watched, her attention momentarily pulled away from the television.

'Don't you bite me!' she heard Maria warn, followed by a sharp shriek.

On her hand, Tilly began to count down from five. Footsteps thundered down the stairs before she had chance to reach two.

'What are you two doing in here?' Her dad's voice boomed far louder than her sister's bickering ever could.

With a sigh, Tilly reached for the remote and stopped the DVD. She wouldn't be able to hear it now with the commotion in the next room.

'The phone doesn't belong to either of you!' he was shouting, using his deepest voice, the one he usually reserved for shouting at his friends across the cluttered factory floor at work. Tilly could hear mumbled complaints.

'I've told you countless times, you're not having mobile phones!'

Tilly could imagine her sisters pouting their lips at him in anger. They asked for mobiles and a computer at least six times a day. Tilly failed to understand why they wanted one so desperately but apparently they were missing out on a whole world of social interaction.

'Dad, Imogen at school has an iPad, a laptop, and an iPhone 5.' Monica would list the luxury items on her painted nails while her Dad would wearily roll his eyes.

'Good for Imogen,' he'd say before turning his attention back to his newspaper.

'Seriously, Dad!' Monica's voice would rise and she'd bunch her hands by her sides in fists.

'You're stifling my development!'

'Yeah!' Maria would eagerly agree. 'We can't go on Facebook, Instagram, Twitter, or Pinterest.' Another list was reeled off with militant precision.

During these conversations, regular as clockwork, Tilly felt for her father. The words her sisters would spout and repeat were as alien to Tilly as they were to him.

Defeated, Tilly went over to the television unit and retrieved her DVD, carefully placing it inside its colourful case. She was about to leave the room when the flimsy door opened once again. This time her dad was looking in at her, his cheeks flushed.

'Are you OK, sweetheart?' he asked amicably. Tilly nodded as she clutched the DVD to her chest.

'Your sisters weren't bothering you, were they?'

Tilly gazed past him. She could see the shadow of the small dining table and the light filtering in from the kitchen, but there was no sign of her sisters.

'I'm OK.' She gave a light shrug.

'Were you watching your movie again?'

'Yes.' This made her face bloom with a bright smile.

'You could certainly teach your sisters a thing or two about getting your money's worth,' her father muttered to himself.

'Daddy, am I too old to be a princess?' Tilly asked directly, her grey eyes wide and expectant. She watched her father give a sigh and run a hand over the back of his neck. He loomed tall on the other side of the room. He was over six feet tall, and long and willowy. He reminded Tilly of the villains in her beloved movies. For some reason, slim men with dark eyes were rarely to be trusted.

'Well, Tilly, you're twelve and you're about to start secondary school. It's around this time that most little girls start acting like, you know, little women.'

Tilly wilted. She was already acutely aware of how different she was from other girls her age. Her friends favoured spending their Saturdays at the shopping centre trying on lipstick they couldn't afford rather than twirling round in princess dresses.

'But you said I'd always be your princess,' Tilly protested. Her father groaned and pushed his hands deep into his pockets.

'Talk to your mother,' he suggested unhelpfully.

'OK,' Tilly chirped brightly before skipping out of the room on her tip toes and heading to her bedroom.

Tilly's bedroom was the smallest room in the house. It was the third bedroom located to the far right of the landing, adjacent to the bathroom. It could barely accommodate the single bunk bed and chest of drawers that occupied it, but Tilly didn't care. Size mattered not. Her bedroom was easily her favourite place in the whole world.

She pushed open the door, which always stubbornly caught on the carpet. Hand drawn signs had been taped up on the outside of the door. Tilly had lovingly penned her name in pink ink and decorated it with butterflies and rainbows.

She glanced across the landing, to the wooden door of the bedroom her sisters begrudgingly shared. The wood was no longer visible – every spare inch was covered in posters of men with chiselled jaws holding guitars or posing in stylish clothes. There was a clear divide in their tastes. Half of the men were groomed and clean shaven while the rest had long, messy hair and holey jeans. Tilly had lost count of the times her sisters had argued over the decoration, and she was grateful no one opposed her glitter-infused signs.

With one huge shove the door opened as wide as it could. It was unable to open all the way since it pressed against the frame of the bunk bed Tilly insisted on having. It had belonged to her sisters and she had inherited it after her eighth birthday.

Once in her room, Tilly closed the door. The back of it was covered in just one poster, which was ripped at the corners and faded, but Tilly refused to take it down. All of her favourite princesses were in the poster, laughing together as though they were having great fun at a party.

Tilly liked to imagine that they were at a sumptuous ball together.

'There.' Tilly slotted her DVD back in with her collection, stacked neatly atop her chest of drawers. The pink furniture was decorated in countless stickers Tilly had accumulated over the years.

Soft pink curtains were already closed over the window which offered an uninspiring view of the estate. The late afternoon sun always shone too brightly into Tilly's room, but with the curtains drawn it bathed the space in a rose-tinted glow.

Sighing contentedly, Tilly moved the two steps required to reach her bed. The bottom level of her bunk bed held dozens of stuffed toys gathered near the pillows. They were all pointed in one specific direction – at the small portable television nestled at the far end of the bed. Tilly's father had promised to buy her a DVD player but it had yet to materialise.

The bed boasted a neatly-tucked princess bed cover. A string of fairy lights dangled across the back wall, sharing the same plug socket as Tilly's television. She loitered for a moment, contemplating snuggling amongst her toys and watching television. But then she considered she'd rather read and in order to do that she had to climb to the top of the tower.

Tilly imagined a beautiful stone tower set amongst an ever green glade where the distant sound of falling water could be heard as soft and alluring as the tinkle of a fairy's bell. Gathering up her glittering dress in her hands, Tilly clenched her jaw in determination. Carefully she climbed, taking care not to lose her grip and tumble down to the rose bushes below. They had been deliberately placed there so their sharp thorns could deter anyone who might dare to disturb the princess.

With a grunt, Tilly reached the top of her tower. From here she could survey her entire Kingdom.

Crossing her legs, Tilly sat on the top level of her bunk bed and glanced up at the glow-in-the-dark plastic stars stuck to the ceiling. On the wall were taped up pictures of huge trees which towered like giants and beautiful rose bushes in vibrant reds and pinks. Tilly had carefully collected them from gardening magazines.

Like every good princess Tilly knew that whilst this tower was her home, she didn't need to wait for a prince to rescue her from it. She had the power to leave as and when she wished.

She leaned back to rummage under her pillow, pulling out a battered copy of Little Women. Though the characters weren't princesses, Tilly still enjoyed reading about them. She opened the book to the page she had previously marked and felt the rose-scented wind filter in through one of the open tower windows.

Savouring the floral scent, Tilly's soft grey eyes began to dance across the words on the page. She tumbled in to the story like Alice down the rabbit hole. Soon she forgot all about the tower and the sea of thorns beneath and thought only of the story unfolding within her little hands.

Tilly gasped as a loud knock shattered her tranquillity. Was the tower under attack? Had someone pressed a battering ram against the great oak doors, determined to reach the princess inside? Her heart racing, Tilly closed her book and placed it back under her pillow. She wondered if she had time to escape. But where would she go? Even if she descended from her tower she risked crossing paths with the potential intruders.

'Here you are.' Her mother's head appeared around the door, flushed from having had to push so hard to get it open. 'Didn't you hear me calling you to come down for dinner?'

Tilly shook her head.

'Well, come on, it's on the table.'

Reluctantly, Tilly climbed down from her tower. It seemed that this time the intruders had won.

Tilly's spirits were lifted when she looked at what awaited her on her plate. There were Potato Smiles, chicken nuggets, and a generous heap of baked beans. Smiling, she sat down and reached for the bottle of ketchup placed at the centre of the table.

'Hands off, squirt!' Her hand was promptly slapped away by Monica, who enthusiastically grabbed the bottle instead.

'Oldest goes first,' she said as she stuck her tongue out at her little sister.

'Girls, can we try to have one civilised dinner?' their father asked.

Monica rolled her eyes as she squirted ketchup over her plate.

'That's enough!' Maria snapped as she snatched the bottle away.

' I wasn't finished!' Monica moaned.

'Yes, you were.'

Beside them, Tilly waited patiently for her turn.

'Dinner looks nice, Mum,' she offered to her mother. Eyes as green as fresh spring grass gazed at her.

'Thank you, sweetheart,' Ivy smiled. Whenever she smiled her features softened in a way that made it look like it was physically impossible for her to ever be mean. But her smile lacked the warmth it used to have. Rays of afternoon sunlight fell on her cheeks, revealing deep set lines and gaunt cheeks.

'Are you not having any nuggets?' Tilly asked in alarm as she noticed that there was steamed fish and vegetables on her mother's plate.

'Not tonight,' Ivy said gently. 'I fancied something a bit different.'

'Give the ketchup to Tilly,' Clive ordered Monica. With an angry sneer she shoved the plastic bottle over to Tilly's side of the table.

Tilly imagined it wasn't a bottle of red sauce but a sacred artefact which was highly coveted within the Kingdom. As she held it above her plate she thought of all the forces who would try to topple her home to lay claim to it.

'I'm so not ready for school on Monday,' Monica announced with disdain.

'Urgh, me neither,' Maria echoed. It was rare for the sisters to agree on anything.

'Make sure you take care of Tilly on Monday.'

Maria scrunched up her face as though she'd smelt something awful.

'What? We're not babysitting the squirt.'

'No way!' Monica echoed between a mouthful of beans.

'You need to look out for Tilly,' their mother insisted, sounding as stern as she could. 'It's her first day at the big school; she'll need you.'

Upon hearing her name thrown around the table Tilly blinked and came back in to the moment. Why were people talking about her?

'Seriously not happening,' Monica said forcefully. 'I'm not being shown up on my first day back.'

'Tilly won't show you up,' Ivy said

defensively, shooting a loving glance in her direction.

'She will!' Maria insisted angrily. 'She'll probably show up dressed like a stupid princess.'

'Don't be silly,' Ivy sighed, 'she'll be wearing her uniform like everyone else.'

Tilly struggled to swallow the piece of chicken lodged in her throat. She had seen the uniform her older sisters wore to school. It consisted of a dark green sweater and black trousers, dull and drab. The sentiment echoed in her mind – 'like everyone else.' Tilly didn't want to be like everyone else. She'd always been different. She'd thought her mother loved that about her.

'Do I have to wear the uniform?' she asked sadly.

'See!' Monica shrieked. 'She already wants to go to school looking like something Disney threw up.'

Tilly defensively drew back. She didn't understand what was wrong with wanting to dress up. Her sisters were always displaying on the outside how they were inside, with heavy black eyeliner and clunky boots. Why couldn't Tilly do the same?

'Yes, you have to wear the uniform,' Tilly's mother explained. Then she shifted her gaze to address her older daughters. 'Stop insulting your sister and finish your dinner.'

Monica mumbled something to herself before shoving a forkful of beans into her mouth.

The rest of dinner was uneventful. Tilly, who was always the last to finish, was polishing off the last of her smiley faces as her father began to collect up the empty plates. Tilly noticed that her mother's plate was still full.

'You should have had what we had,' she told her mother earnestly. Ivy looked at her plate.

'I guess I'm just not that hungry,' she explained. Tilly shrugged and went back to finishing her dinner.

Tilly skipped through the lounge, eager to get back to her tower, but she stopped when she clocked the pile of washing crammed in a plastic basket beside the sofa, waiting for her mother to iron her way through it while watching Poldark. At the top of the pile was a pale green shirt and a pair of smart black trousers. Tilly could see from the size that it was her school uniform. Dread began to close around her like a fist, each finger squeezing unpleasantly against her. Secondary school terrified her. It was her sister's territory, a place where girls chased after boys and teachers gave out detention as though it were candy. It wasn't a place where fairy tales could flourish. Swallowing nervously, Tilly turned away and hurried up the stairs, more eager than ever to lock herself away.

A great storm had occurred out at sea. Ships had succumbed to the relentless waves which burst against their boughs and people feared that more souls would be lost. A dark, unforgiving sky hung ominously above the water.

The captain of the fleet's remaining ship did his best to hold steady at the wheel. He had the most precious cargo on board: the princess. He knew the entire Kingdom depended on her safe passage home. Cold water flung against him but still he remained at the wheel, his jaw clenched with steely determination. He'd weathered worse storms. He'd make it back to harbour no matter what.

'Tilly, come on! You've been in there

forever!' a voice whined through the bathroom door, forcing Tilly to put down her plastic ship and let it fend for itself amongst the strawberry-scented bubbles.

'I'm in the bath!' she shouted back. She heard Monica groan on the other side of the door.

'Ten minutes, squirt. Then I'm coming in, so you'd better be decent.'

Tilly sank further into the lukewarm water. She didn't want to rush her bath. To do so would edge her one step closer to the following Monday morning and the first day at a new school. Her stomach churned uneasily at the thought.

As much as she wanted to stay in the tub she knew her sister would make good on her threat and come barging in, allowing all of the trapped warm air to spew out on to the landing. With a sigh, Tilly climbed out and wrapped herself in a grey towel which had once been white.

The storm for her sailors had now cleared and there were only blue skies ahead as they continued their journey to the Kingdom.

Tilly did her best to delay going to bed. She dried her hair by the fire and watched television with her mother while she did the ironing. She offered twice to hoover or do some washing up but Ivy just shook her head and smiled.

'Try to relax,' she said. 'You've got a big day ahead of you tomorrow.'

Frowning, Tilly tried not to think of the printed class schedule shoved into the front pocket of her bright pink backpack. A day of science and French awaited her. But it wouldn't just be the classes that were unfamiliar. It was all going to be foreign. She'd be walking down corridors she'd not seen before amongst a sea of unknown faces.

She'd passed by her new school numerous times when her sisters had required collecting or dropping off. It was a huge, grey building which cut an ominous shape against the sky. It looked more like a prison than a school.

It was easy to imagine that the school was an elaborate castle for some villain. To Tilly it was obvious that nothing good could reside within. It was as if it had been built out of a dreary Wednesday afternoon. Everything about the school embodied drudgery and dismay.

'Mum, do I really have to go?' Tilly asked her mother in the vain hope that perhaps her parents had changed their minds and decided to recognise her as the princess she truly was.

'Yes, you really have to go,' Ivy stated, her eyes never leaving the handsome man who had appeared on the television screen.

Tilly made a sound of disappointment.

'It's only five years; it'll be over before you know it.'

Five years. Tilly felt her throat start to constrict. Five years felt like a lifetime. She couldn't even begin to imagine how long that really was, but it felt infinite.

Tilly's spirits failed to rise as she climbed the familiar path to her tower. She was thankful to lie down and try to imagine herself somewhere far, far away. But despite the darkness, the street light just beyond her window was on and it shone bright enough to illuminate the outline of shapes gathered around the room. Tilly could make out the uniform hanging on her chest of drawers. It had no colour in the darkness but it looked just as awful as it did in the harsh light of day. She didn't want to wear it, didn't want to attend the school where her sisters already went.

They knew their way around, where to avoid, and who to make friends with but they wouldn't share such hard-earned secrets with Tilly. She knew they expected her to fend for herself just as they once had.

How had the summer holidays slipped by so quickly? Tilly thought that six weeks would last forever. Yet the days had grown sharper and trees were already starting to cautiously shed their leaves. Autumn was growing closer and with it, the start of a new school year. All Tilly wanted to do was curl into a ball and cry herself to sleep. She wasn't ready for this adventure, for this meteoric change about to occur. She needed to be the princess in the tower, safe and far removed from the real world.

But her dreams didn't come to save her. Instead, she gazed bleakly at the shadow of her waiting uniform before she finally fell asleep.

A Pumpkin for a Carriage

'No way,' Monica shook her mane and pursed her glossy lips.

'Yeah, Dad – not happening,' Maria agreed.

Tilly stood awkwardly beside them on the street outside their house where her dad was waiting in the family car. She tentatively eyed their uniforms which, whilst the same as hers, looked wildly different on them.

Monica had rolled up the sleeves of her jumper and wore silver bangles on her wrist which gave a musical tinkle each time she gestured. Her regulation trousers seemed to pinch in tightly at the waist and give her a flattering silhouette. She wore heavy black boots and her dark hair cascaded down her back like a gothic waterfall.

Maria had also made alterations to her uniform. Her tie was short and fat instead of long. Her hair was gathered atop her head in an oversized bun and studs lined the length of her ear. Both sisters had on too much eyeliner, which made any dark looks they gave even more sinister.

In contrast, Tilly wore her brand new uniform exactly as the regulations stipulated. Her tie was tucked into the band of her trousers, she wore flat black ballet pumps with black socks, and her brown hair was pulled into a long plait. The only flair of individuality she'd dared bring to the outfit was her bright pink backpack adorned with a glitter-infused image of a smiling princess.

Tilly had heard her sisters scoff in disapproval when they saw it. They both carried more fashionable shoulder bags adorned with badges which publically announced which TV shows and bands they favoured.

'I'm giving you girls a lift to school,' Clive repeated. 'I don't have to be at work until nine so come on, get in.'

Tilly immediately approached the car but her sisters remained rooted where they stood.

'No.' Monica was shaking her head, her eyes wide.

'No offence, Dad, but I wouldn't be seen dead in that thing.' Maria added with a lift of a perfectly-shaped eyebrow.

The family car was by no means a Porsche. It was a much more humble model and time had not been kind to it. Most of the paintwork had been replaced by the deep red of rust and its design was so old that you had to wind down the windows and lock each door individually.

'Stop being precious,' Clive scolded, growing impatient. 'It's Tilly's first day.'

'Seriously, you'd be better off walking,' Monica told her. Tilly felt like she was about to be torn in half. One part of her wanted to climb into the musty-smelling car like her dad wanted, but another, more timid, part of her wanted to listen to her sister and heed her advice.

'Yeah, roll up in that banger and it's social suicide,' Maria agreed, folding her arms across her chest.

'Fine, walk, whatever,' Clive sighed. 'But Tilly doesn't care about silly things like being popular. You just want to get to school on time, don't you, sweetheart?'

Tilly looked up at her father. She could see the tense lines around his eyes though he was trying to smile. If she walked away now she knew he'd feel like he'd lost all of his daughters to adolescence. Without saying another word she climbed in the car.

'Your funeral.' Monica waved a hand at her, her bangles providing a soft accompaniment to her words. Arm in arm, her sisters turned away from the house and began walking down the street, their heads bent in close as they gossiped about the day ahead.

'You've always been the sensible one,' Tilly's father smiled at her as he climbed into the driver's seat.

'You changed your shift at work on purpose, didn't you?'

'Yeah,' Clive gave a sad smile as he turned the key in the ignition. After repeating this several times the engine reluctantly spluttered to life.

'Your mum wanted one of us to see you off on your first day.'

'Is she still sleeping?' Tilly glanced back at their house and the largest window upstairs where the curtains were drawn. She wondered if she willed it hard enough they might part and her mother's smiling face would appear to wave her off. But the curtains remained drawn. It was strange that her mother wouldn't get up to see her off. At breakfast, everyone else had been so busy pretending it was normal for her to sleep in that Tilly hadn't dared to question it.

'Yeah, she is. She's just a bit run down.'

'There are a lot of colds going around,' Tilly commented. Something about what she'd said made her dad smile.

'What?'

'Sometimes you're very much my little girl. And other times you say things that make you sound so grown up.'

'What's grown up about what I said?'

'Nothing.' Her dad shook his head as he turned out of their street. 'It's just what I'd expect to hear from someone at work, not my little girl.'

Tilly leaned back contentedly in her seat, ignoring how rigid and uncomfortable it felt. She liked it when Dad called her his little girl. There was something safe and comforting about it.

27

The drive to school only took ten minutes. As the car weaved through town it passed near the centre of Dullerton, which had once been thriving but was now mostly derelict. It had been in its prime several decades ago. Tilly often heard her parents reminiscing about how things had once been. How the town used to feel lively and busy and that there was always enough work. Now jobs were scarce and the town was slowly succumbing to decay. Each time someone left Dullerton they never came back –they had no reason to.

The car paused at the traffic lights and Tilly looked out through the smeared window and saw the local park where she'd blissfully spent hours as a child. Back then it had felt like a sprawling wilderness, an enchanted forest. At the centre of it there was a glittering gold carousel which Tilly could ride for the price of an ice cream. She loved getting inside one of the ornate carriages and going round and round as the carousel music played. Each time she passed her mother she'd wave wildly as she pretended that she was on her way to a royal ball. The horses became free from their poles and galloped beside her carriage, their manes flowing in the breeze. The sound of hooves thundering against the ground could be heard from miles around. People would lean out of their windows and exclaim that the princess must be coming.

But like the rest of Dullerton, the carousel had fallen on hard times and had ceased running several years ago. Now nature was doing her best to reclaim it. Weeds sprouted up within the carriages and trees greedily stretched their long branches underneath the main canopy.

From the car, Tilly could make out the raised dome of the carousel in the park. It wasn't as bright as it had once been. Years ago it had glittered as brightly as a star, blinking out to nearby children to take a ride. Now the dome had been dulled by time and weathered away to a shadow of its former self. She raised her fingertips against the window and looked out longingly towards the park. How she wished she could climb into her carriage and be swept away to a faraway Kingdom.

'I forgot how bad the school traffic can be,' her dad moaned as he managed to find a space and haul the car onto the curb. The pavement was a sea of green as hundreds of students congregated together like migrating birds heading towards the great stone structure which loomed before them.

'Dad, do I have to go?' Tilly sunk into her seat. She felt sick, as though she'd taken one too many rides on her beloved carousel.

'I'm afraid so, Tilly,' her dad said as he leaned over her to open her car door. The morning air gushed inside, offering a brief respite from the overwhelming musty odour which lingered in the car.

'I don't want to,' Tilly announced stubbornly, clutching her backpack to her chest as though it were a shield.

'Sorry, sweetheart, but you have to. Besides, your mum will want to hear all about your day later. You don't want to disappoint her, do you?'

Tilly chewed her lip as she looked over the dashboard at the ominous building. It was a black hole on the landscape. Once someone went in youthful and brimming with optimism they never came back out the same way.

'Come on, Tilly, I need to move the car. Other people want the space.' An angry edge had crept into her dad's previously warm tone.

'OK.' Tilly forced herself to leave. She

positioned her backpack firmly on both shoulders before waving farewell.

He offered her only a brief nod, his attention already consumed with manoeuvring out into the throng of traffic.

Taking a deep breath, Tilly forced herself to walk in the same direction as the other green jumpers. People were talking excitedly, catching up on their summer adventures. Tilly scanned the crowd for something she could draw comfort from – perhaps another bright pink bag with a smiling princess on it. But all the students around her were like her sisters. They even smelled like them, as though a florist had collided with a sweet shop.

'You can do this,' Tilly told herself. All she'd wanted to do was cry. Ever since breakfast when her mum had failed to materialise, she'd yearned to curl up atop her tower and never come back down. She'd needed to see her mother's face, to hear her soft voice.

'Hey, watch it.' A ginger-haired boy wearing too much hair gel turned and scowled at Tilly as he fiercely pushed past her. Tilly's cheeks started to burn but she managed to keep walking. As she approached the green iron gates she was shoved a few more times. People pushed her aside like she was nothing more than an unwanted condiment on the table. After one particularly forceful encounter, Tilly almost lost her footing.

Finally she reached the main yard and started to spot the occasional familiar face – students also embarking on their first day. Tilly felt a wave of relief sweep through her. She wanted to run to them, to skip over to Kate, Sophie, and Claire and ask how their summer had been, just as she'd heard others do on her walk to the gate. But they didn't look like they had at junior school. Tilly stopped short when she noticed their sleek new hairstyles and shoulder bags they had casually slung across them. Gripping the straps of her own backpack she remembered how they used to tease her for being childish. Would they seek her out only to mock her in her pristine uniform?

'Oh, Tilly.' It was too late. They had spotted her. It was Kate who had addressed her. She had eyes the colour of ice and was just as cold. She tossed her white-blonde hair over her shoulder and not very discreetly nudged Sophie standing beside her. Sophie already towered above her friends and she gazed down at Tilly with a sinister smile.

'Hey, Tilly.'

'Hi.' Tilly hovered nervously. She felt them crowd around her like witches before a cauldron.

'Nice backpack,' Kate laughed cruelly. 'We're in secondary school now, Tilly. You might want to think about growing up a bit.'

The others cackled and Tilly edged away, her hands tightening against her bright pink straps. More than anything she wanted to be in her tower, where no one could get to her.

As the day wore on, it didn't improve. Tilly attended registration where she was handed a worryingly vague map of the school and her timetable. Each minute of the day was accounted for, boxed away into the neat little spaces. Tilly swallowed down her sense of dread as she read through her weekly schedule. She'd be studying science, French, mathematics, English language and literature. All the subjects blurred into one giant, never-ending box of allocated studying time.

Pushing her timetable away, Tilly tilted her head to gaze outside through the large window she was sat beside. It was hard to tell where the grey sky ended and the tarmacked sea of the playground began. They blended together seamlessly, making the entire landscape look like it was doused in a dense fog.

Tilly wondered what was happening back at her old school and her heart tightened in her chest. She'd liked her junior school. The walls were painted vibrant shades of the rainbow and the building was spread out over one level – there were no one-way staircase systems to navigate. Tilly's best friend, Josephine, had been there. Together they'd discuss what books they were reading. On weekends they had sleepovers and watched their favourite Disney films back to back.

When summer started, Josephine and her family moved away. Her dad had taken a job in London. Tilly angrily knotted her hands together as she bent her head towards her chest. Josephine might as well have moved to the moon. If only she was there with Tilly, then this new, big school might not seem so scary.

'Let's see what classes you have.' Tilly had unwillingly ended up sat beside Kate, who had dropped down beside her just as the bell rang, her two cronies to her right.

Kate reached for the timetable with her neon pink nails before Tilly could protest.

'Ooh,' Kate cooed dramatically as she showed the piece of paper to her friends.

'Someone's a swot,' Sophie commented.

'Am not,' Tilly mumbled, refusing to look at them.

'You are too!' Kate insisted in her annoyingly shrill voice. 'Look at this,' she jabbed a nail at the timetable, 'you've got higher maths and English.'

'Swot,' Sophie repeated with a smug smile.

'Give that back,' Tilly ordered, hoping she sounded braver than she felt. Kate's blue eyes sparkled teasingly but she thankfully relented and handed Tilly her timetable back.

'You can be such a baby,' she said with a roll of her eyes as Tilly shoved the paper inside her backpack.

'Girls,' a stern voice boomed from the front of the class. They all straightened up in their seats and looked towards the whiteboard where Miss Havishorn was standing, her hands on her large hips. Her red-stained lips were drawn in a tight, angry line.

'You're supposed to be writing down what you want to achieve during this academic year, not talking amongst yourselves. Gossiping can wait until break time.'

Miss Havishorn was to be Tilly's form tutor. She was a plump woman with permed hair and pretty eyes hidden behind tortoiseshell glasses. When Tilly had first seen her she had hoped she would be kind, but the moment one of the unruly boys in the class spoke out of turn, Miss Havishorn showed she was a force to be reckoned with.

Furtively, Tilly pulled her notebook from her backpack, along with her pink pencil case on which several princesses were pictured. She heard Kate snicker when she saw it but refused to give her the satisfaction of reacting. Tilly pulled out one of her favourite pens and looked down at the crisp, new page in her notebook.

The title for the task was neatly written on the whiteboard in Miss Havishorn's tidy handwriting:

My Goals
for This School Year

Tilly took her time writing down the title. Beside her she could see Kate and her friends eagerly scribbling down long paragraphs. Tilly looked back out the window, at the bleak world which she'd have to inhabit five days out of the week. It felt like she had journeyed into some deep, dark world far removed from the one she knew in her beloved tower. She should be on some fabled quest to destroy a tainted ring or vanquish some evil queen. Why else would she have to venture to such an oppressive place?

The bleak, rain-stained school walls were no place to house a princess. Tilly drummed her pen against her notebook and wondered what Josephine's school was like. It was private. Did that mean that she'd have bright walls and classrooms bursting with colour?

'Five minutes and then you'll be sharing what you've written with the rest of the class.' Miss Havishorn's voice blasted through the room, over the heads of her students and into Tilly's thoughts.

Blinking, Tilly looked down at her blank page. What were her goals for the school year? She didn't feel like she had any. She was just trying to make it through her first day, not even thinking about the year ahead. But everyone else was scrawling away in their notebooks, clearly brimming with ideas for their future.

Taking a quick intake of breath, Tilly wrote down her main goal in one simple sentence.

'OK, let's go from the back,' Miss Havishorn gazed expectantly through her glasses towards Tilly's table. 'You thought sitting at the back would spare you; think again.'

Tilly's shoulders slumped and she sank as low as the stiff plastic chair would allow.

'I'll go first.' Kate smiled vapidly at the teacher.

'Very good.'

'My goals for this school year are to join the netball team. To learn French ...' Kate paused and flirtatiously caught the eye of the some of the nearby boys, which Miss Havishorn didn't seem to notice. '… To make new friends, and be the best student I can possibly be,' Kate concluded as she flicked her hair over her shoulder and shrugged with faux modesty. Tilly wasn't sure if it was her words or the overpowering stench of Kate's cheap perfume but she suddenly felt nauseous.

'Great goals.' Miss Havishorn nodded in approval though she did not smile. Tilly was starting to wonder if she ever did.

'And you …'

'Tilly.'

'Tilly?' Miss Havishorn frowned as she repeated Tilly's name. She scrunched up her plump cheeks as though she'd eaten something unpleasant.

'What's that short for?'

'Matilda, Miss.'

'Matilda, that's a lovely name. That's what you should be known as at school. It's the name your parents gave you and you should be proud to use it.'

Tilly blinked. What was wrong with her regular name, Tilly? It was a part of who she was, of her identity.

'So, Matilda, what did you write?'

Tilly felt words trying to push their way out of her mouth, words that weren't written down in her notebook. She wanted to tell Miss Havishorn that it was Tilly, not Matilda. But instead she politely read the sentence she'd penned.

'My goal for this school year is to survive.'

Miss Havishorn drew her eyebrows together and stared at Tilly.

'Is that it?' she demanded.

'That's it.'

'But my dear girl, you don't want to just survive whilst you are here; you want to thrive!'

Tilly opened her mouth to object. She was more than happy to merely just survive, but then the school bell rang out, stealing her words.

'OK, off to your next class. I'll see you after lunch for afternoon registration.' Miss Havishorn had to shout to be heard over the excited chatter which now rumbled through the classroom. Tilly stood up and hurriedly put her notebook and pencil case back in her backpack. According to her timetable she now had French, and the language block was on the other side of the school. She had no idea how long it would take her to find it.

Tilly quietly followed Kate and her friends towards the classroom door, but just as she was about to cross the threshold to the bustling corridor, Kate spun around.

'FYI, Matilda,' her eyes gleamed with pleasure as she overly pronounced Tilly's full name, 'little girls don't survive here, so it looks like you won't be making your goal for the year.'

Kate was laughing as she linked arms with Sophie and Claire and sauntered down the corridor. Tilly watched them leave, imagining them as wicked witches.

'So, how was school?' Tilly turned as she closed the front door in the direction of the voice and saw her mother peeling potatoes by the kitchen sink. Beneath the garish glow of the strip light on the ceiling, her skin looked almost translucent.

Tilly did her best to remain glued together, but she could feel the seams coming unstuck. She dropped her backpack to the ground with a soft thud and looked longingly at the staircase.

'Tilly?' Her mother had put down the potato she was holding, her voice warm with concern.

Tilly bolted up the stairs, bounding up two at a time despite her little legs. She ran straight for her bedroom and climbed into her tower. She could feel the wolves – which were Kate, Sophie, and Claire – snapping at her ankles. Once safely within her tower, Tilly breathed a sigh of relief. She could hear the gentle lilt of birdsong instead of the urban soundtrack of car engines and horns.

Her heart began to calm. Tilly buried her head in her pillow and screamed, letting the fabric absorb the sound.

'Tilly?' The door opened and her mother stepped inside. The borders of the tower had been breached but Tilly didn't care. She remained face down on her bed.

'Hey, Tilly.' Her mother was tall enough to reach the top of the tower. She lifted a hand and nudged her daughter's side.

'Was it really so bad?' she asked gently.

Sniffling, Tilly rolled over to look at her mum. She wiped a hand across her eyes and nodded.

'It was really bad.'

'Oh, sweetheart.'

The bunk bed groaned as her mother climbed the tower. Once at the top, she could only lie down. She nuzzled up beside Tilly and planted a soft kiss on her forehead.

'Do you want to talk about it?'

'No.' Tilly didn't want to think about it, let alone talk about it. But the worst part was that the next day she had to live through it again. It was like she'd unwittingly walked into some never-ending punishment. She kept telling herself that all princesses go through troubled times but they aren't left beneath the ocean or scrubbing floors forever. They eventually earn their happily ever after.

'It'll get better, Tilly.' Her mother stroked her head. The soothing sensation made Tilly's eyes feel heavy.

'My form tutor wants to call me Matilda,' she muttered softly.

'But you're Tilly,' her mother instantly objected.

'I know.' Fresh tears dropped down Tilly's cheeks.

'It's just a name,' her mother continued. 'A Tilly by any other name would be just as sweet.'

Tilly smiled as her mum kissed her forehead again.

'Do I really have to go back?' Tilly wondered forlornly.

'I'm afraid so.' Her mother was getting up now, wincing as she manoeuvred her long body back over the side of the tower.

'I'm making fish and chips for dinner – your favourite. Will that cheer you up?'

Tilly nodded eagerly as her stomach gave a long growl. In her distress she had failed to notice how hungry she was.

'Sounds like someone needs feeding,' her mother laughed. She was at the bedroom door when she paused and glanced back up at her daughter.

'You know, no matter what anyone says to you at school or anywhere else, you'll always be Tilly to me, sweetheart.'

'Thanks, Mum.'

Tilly clung to her mother's words whilst she tried to ignore the ever-present terror of the school day that awaited her.

All I Want is Your Voice

The periodic table glared out at Tilly from across the room.

Her tall, bearded science teacher was directing his marker pen towards the table. 'This, you must commit to memory.'

Tilly's eyes widened. The periodic table was huge, containing an assortment of abbreviations Tilly knew she'd never be able to fully memorise, not if she stared at it for a hundred years. She could sense the apprehension of her fellow students in the room, so at least she wasn't alone in her thoughts.

'You each have a copy.' Tilly's teacher lowered his pen to adjust the ill-fitting waistcoat he was wearing. 'Every night I want you to get it out and study it.'

Tilly looked down at her own miniature version. The amount of information she needed to absorb seemed even more daunting when shrunk and crammed on to a sheet of A4 paper. But as her eyes scanned the boxes she recognised some of the elements, like gold and silver. She ran a finger over them. Crowns were made of gold because it was precious, and in her Kingdom the tips of arrows were dipped in silver so when they were fired they glinted majestically in the sun, seeking to blind their opponent.

'Your homework this week is to learn the table by heart.' Her teacher's voice grew louder as he had to fight to be heard over the shrill of the bell.

Blinking, Tilly came back to reality. All thoughts of gold and silver dissolved and she was left in the grey of the science lab, the only source of colour provided by her bright backpack. Students were already heading out the door, eager to escape in to the bustling corridors. Tilly packed away her belongings before hurrying out after them.

Tilly ate her lunch alone. Most people brought in money so they could go to the canteen and buy something hot for dinner but Tilly preferred to have her packed lunch. It was what she'd had back at junior school.

She'd tucked herself away at the far end of one of the long plastic tables which lined the dinner hall. A cacophony of sound bounced around the large space as children chattered. Tilly zoned them all out. She carefully pulled out her pink princess lunch box and cracked the lid. The smell that wafted up was full of a thousand pleasant memories.

Lunch consisted of a cheese sandwich on brown bread, a packet of salt and vinegar crisps, a banana, and a carton of orange juice. As Tilly looked at her carefully arranged items she gave a wistful sigh. If only Josephine was here. They would swap items and stories about their morning. But without her friend by her side, Tilly was very much alone. She reached for her sandwich and as she lifted it from the lunch box she noticed the slip of paper folded beneath it. Tilly unfolded it, instantly recognising her mother's neat handwriting.

Have a good day sweetheart. Things will get better at school, I promise..

I love you.

Mum xxxx

Tilly re-read the note over and over until her vision threatened to blur with tears. Then she carefully folded it back up and placed it back into her lunch box before biting into her sandwich.

'Are you actually eating out here alone?'

Tilly smelt Kate before she saw her. The sugary scent of her perfume was so overwhelming that Tilly struggled to take in a clean breath of air. She dropped her sandwich back into her lunch box and hastily wiped her eyes in case any tears had fallen without her noticing.

'Look, girls.' Kate was gliding up towards Tilly, wearing her standard supercilious smirk.

'This is what it looks like to be a total loser.'

'Pretty pathetic if you ask me,' Sophie commented, folding her arms across her chest.

'Don't have your buddy Josephine to sit and giggle with now, do you?' Kate asked, each word dripping with spite.

'Little Matilda is all alone.' Kate tilted her head to the side and wiped away fake tears.

Taking a deep breath, Tilly thought of the note. Even though she felt alone, she wasn't. There was someone back home who loved her dearly and she clung to that.

Growing bored of the conversation, Kate flipped her hair over her shoulder and began to walk off.

'See you later, loser.' She tossed the goodbye to Tilly with a brief backward glance. Tilly watched them leave and when she was certain they were out of sight she quickly retrieved her mum's note and re-read it half a dozen more times.

'Oh my God, could you believe Mr Rogers in maths this morning?' Kate was talking loudly to her friends as they walked into registration. She always talked loudly to ensure everyone could hear her.

'I know,' Sophie instantly agreed. 'He is totally lame.'

'Right?'

Tilly drew her arms around herself and looked out of the window. The last thing she wanted was to engage Kate and her friends in conversation. She was still feeling fragile.

'And to think he threatened me with detention,' Kate scoffed as she sat down, bringing with her a cloud of sickly sweet air. Whatever perfume she wore, it was much more offensive than what Tilly's sisters doused themselves in each morning.

'He's lame!' Sophie insisted again, stretching out her long legs beneath the table.

'Completely lame.' Claire spoke up from the end of the table.

Tilly was still staring out of the window. She imagined a white steed galloping in to the school yard, its hooves clattering noisily against the sun-bleached tarmac; its mane glistened in the sunlight, as did the armour worn by the knight riding it. As the horse reared up majestically he'd lift up the metal visor and find Tilly staring out through the window. He'd beckon to her with a gloved hand. At first Tilly would resist, but then he'd remove his helmet to reveal a tumble of thick, dark hair which fell over his bright green eyes. He'd beckon for her again and the horse would bay and Tilly would know they were there to save her. She'd throw on her backpack, dash outside and never look back.

A dreamy smile pulled on her lips as Miss Havishorn began addressing the class.

'What are you smiling about?' Kate asked, her voice now a sharp whisper.

'Huh?' Tilly pulled her gaze from the window and looked at Kate, who was frowning at her. She glanced quickly back towards the now-empty school yard. The steed and her rescuer were gone.

'You're smiling like a weirdo,' Kate hissed. 'Why?'

Tilly could feel her cheeks starting to burn.

'I wasn't smiling,' she whispered back, aware of how lame her response was.

'Liar,' Kate seethed.

'I'm … I'm not lying,' Tilly felt like she was being unwittingly backed into a very tight corner. She wanted to place her backpack protectively against her chest.

'Girls!' Miss Havishorn was staring them down from the front of the classroom. 'This is not the time for a chat. That's what your lunch break is for.'

'It was Matilda, Miss,' Kate declared smugly as she folded her arms and lifted her chin. 'I told her to be quiet but she wouldn't shut up.'

'That's not true!' Tilly was appalled at how Kate could lie so blatantly.

'It is. You're always talking!' Kate was smirking, savouring the sensation of all eyes being on her. 'You're a blabbermouth.'

'And you're a liar,' Tilly told her contritely.

'Enough!' Miss Havishorn's nostrils were flared as she began advancing towards them, her large frame struggling to fit between the aisle created between the desks. 'Get your school diaries out now, both of you!'

Tilly blanched. She knew why teachers requested a student's diary – it was either to offer them a Merit stamp for work well done, or the much less appealing Detention stamp for when they had behaved badly. Tilly had only seen one Detention passed out so far, to a boy called Stuart who had muttered an expletive about his teacher not quietly enough.

'It was Matilda's fault!' Kate declared in a shrill, alarmed tone.

'School diaries, now,' Miss Havishorn demanded.

Tilly quietly reached into her backpack whilst Kate continued to protest.

'I don't see why I should be punished,' she lamented. 'I was only telling Matilda to be quiet.'

'If you don't give me your school diary this instant I'll be giving you an after-school detention rather than a lunch time one.'

The mood in the room became icy as Tilly felt her entire body freeze with fear. She was getting a lunch time detention. This couldn't be happening. Detentions were something her sisters collected for wearing too much make up or back-chatting a teacher. It didn't happen to Tilly – she was a good student.

'Diaries.' Miss Havishorn was growing increasingly impatient. Sheepishly, Tilly handed hers over, as did Kate.

'Let this be a lesson to you both,' Miss Havishorn was saying as she found the relevant week in their diaries and issued the detention. Tilly swallowed nervously as she watched the stamp get pushed down onto her pristine page. She hadn't even earned a Merit stamp yet. The first imprint was a negative one. She suddenly felt like a giant D had been branded onto her forehead.

Once the detentions had been issued for the following day, Miss Havishorn returned the diaries to their owners.

'You'll pay for this,' Kate whispered when she was certain that Miss Havishorn was far enough away not to hear.

Tilly was hurriedly putting her diary away. She would indeed pay for receiving a detention on her second day, but it wasn't Kate's retribution she feared. It was what would happen at home.

As the bell rang, Tilly couldn't leave her chair fast enough. She darted into the hallway, her mind an indecipherable collection of panicked questions. Kate didn't make any efforts to follow her, instead flanked by her friends, who were already offering words of consolation – most of them barbed comments about Tilly.

Head down, Tilly ran down the corridor, ignoring the school's no running policy. She didn't care any more. She already had a detention: a giant black mark against her name. She was about to head down the stairs towards the English Block when a firm hand gripped her shoulder.

'Hey, where's the fire?'

Standing still, Tilly realised how fast she must have been going as she was now breathing hard. She was surprised to see Monica towering over her, one hand on Tilly's shoulder.

'You shouldn't run,' Monica said sternly, her tone making her sound more fifty than fifteen.

'Besides, you're not even late yet.'

Tilly almost shook with relief to see a familiar face. She wanted to remain composed, to show her sister how she was coping with this frightening new environment, but like an undercooked pastry she instantly crumbled. Hot tears began to fall down her cheeks. Monica sent a panicked glance around before firmly guiding her sister down the stairs towards a quiet corridor where they were alone.

'What's the matter?' Monica's voice was softer than usual. 'It's really not so bad here once you get used to it.'

'I ...' Tilly wiped the sleeve of her jumper across her damp cheeks. 'I got a detention.'

'What?' Monica stiffened with surprise. 'Are you serious?'

Tilly could only nod as more tears fell from her eyes.

'Argh, Tilly.' Monica fished a tissue from her pocket and reached for Tilly's chin, gripping it and closely studying her face. She began to wipe away as many tears as her tissue would allow.

'Don't stress about it now, OK? Crying here is like bleeding out in shark-infested waters. The moment people smell a drop they'll be drawn to you and rip you to shreds.'

Tilly nodded and willed herself to stop crying.

'Whatever you did, I'm sure you didn't mean it.' Monica was still wiping her face. With her eyebrows drawn together in concentration in the dim light of the corridor, she looked like a younger, more made up version of their mother. The resemblance made Tilly's breath catch in her throat.

'There.' Monica cast a critical eye over Tilly and stepped back, placing her hands on her sister's shoulders. 'Forget about the detention and just make it to the end of the day, OK?'

'What will Mum and Dad say?'

'They've got bigger things to worry about. Besides, I've had loads of detentions, so don't worry about it.' Monica gave a shrug. Tilly still looked like a startled rabbit caught in headlights.

'But you're like, the Golden Child, so they might be pissed off but you can deal with that.' She squeezed Tilly's shoulders. 'You really need to toughen up, squirt, or else this world will just chew you up and spit you out.'

Tilly hung her head shamefully.

'Look, I need to go before someone sees us together.' Monica was glancing warily at the corridor ahead as students were starting to filter in. 'Be tough,' she offered, before releasing Tilly and darting back the way she had come.

The sun was shining as Tilly's dad drove her home, which meant he was able to wind down the windows and turn up the stereo, which was currently playing one of his favourite cassette tapes. Tilly did her best to tune the music out but she knew each song by heart. Whenever she heard it, it reminded her of the car journey down to Cornwall where the tape had been turned over so many times she lost count. Annoyingly, her parents hadn't thought to bring more than one cassette with them for a nine-hour journey, and so Tilly would forever be word perfect on Phil Collins songs. At first she had been quite fond of them, but now they just reminded her of being stuck in gridlock traffic and desperately needing to pee.

'And I remember ...' Her dad was enthusiastically singing along as he tapped the wheel, not caring about the glances he drew from students walking along the street. Tilly sunk down in her seat hoping no one recognised her as he continued to sing along.

Once the song ended, he didn't let the tape play on; he rewound it back to the start again.

'I don't know why but I love listening to this song when the sun shines,' he muttered merrily to himself. 'Strange, huh?'

'Yeah,' she said softly. And it was strange, given the song was about someone drowning, a fact her sisters had smugly shared with her during the never-ending Cornwall car journey. While her dad was distracted by his music he hadn't noticed her red eyes and sour expression. Nor had he asked about her day, which meant her detention got to remain a secret for a little while longer.

The house smelt of roast chicken as soon as Tilly walked through the front door. Normally she'd take a moment to inhale the aroma but instead she quickly stalked off upstairs. She needed to avoid her mother; she'd be the one to ask prying questions about her day, ones she wouldn't be able to evade.

Tilly was almost within the safety of her tower when the bedroom door creaked open and her mum walked in.

'How was school?'

With a sigh, Tilly climbed back down the metal ladder and looked at her mother. She looked tired even though she wasn't working – she'd been let go from the office where she worked as a secretary. Tilly really didn't understand what could be making her so tired all the time.

'School was … fine.' Tilly searched for a reasonable response.

'It was?' Hope sparkled in her mum's eyes, restoring some the colour to her washed out cheeks.

'Yeah,' Tilly nodded confidently. 'It was.'

'Oh, good.' Her mum bent down to kiss her cheek. Her lips were cold even though her cheeks were flushed. 'I'm glad to hear that. Dinner will be ready in an hour, OK?'

'OK.'

Tilly dove into her cooked dinner. She'd been yearning for it since she got home. Even her mother's plate was piled high with meat, vegetables, roasted potatoes and gravy.

'How come we're having a roast dinner today?' Maria asked, playing with her food.

'Yeah, it's not Sunday,' Monica agreed.

'I thought it would be a nice change.' Their mother smiled. 'And I know it's one of Tilly's favourite meals.'

'Oh.' Monica glanced in her sister's direction. 'So you're not mad then?'

Tilly ceased chewing. The meat in her mouth, which had previously been delicious, now felt dry and heavy.

'Mad?' Ivy Tilly's mum offered her daughter a bemused smile.

'Yeah,' Monica nodded towards Tilly, 'because of the detention.'

Tilly felt the white hot heat of the interrogation lamp suddenly burn in her face.

'What detention?' Their mother offered the question first to Monica, then to Tilly.

'Yes, what detention?' Clive put down his knife and fork, and gazed at his youngest daughter, anger already simmering behind his grey eyes.

'It's …' Tilly squirmed beneath the intensity of their gaze. All eyes at the dinner table were on her. 'I got a detention for talking during registration.' She chose to be honest. To drop the bombshell as calmly as possible and hope it didn't explode too violently in her face.

'Well.' Her father was caressing his freshly-shaven cheeks, clearly searching for what to say.

'Tilly, I'm very disappointed in you.' It was her mother's words that pounded against her chest with the power of a wrecking ball.

Disappointment – that was always worse than anger.

'We'd expect this sort of behaviour from your sisters, but not you,' Clive added as Monica and Maria shared a disdainful look.

'Why were you talking in registration?' her mother asked softly.

'I … I didn't mean to.' Tilly nervously knitted her hands together. 'The girl sat next to me,

Kate, she was the one who was talking.'

'Kate?' A bulb went off in Tilly's father's mind as he straightened and looked away, searching the space in the room for something.

'Kate Oswald?' he asked.

'Yes,' Tilly was nodding.

'Why were you sat next to Kate Oswald?' her father demanded. 'That girl is nothing but trouble. Her father works with me and he's always moaning about her.'

'Yes, I remember her from your junior school.' Ivy was nodding in agreement. 'She was always such a naughty girl. You don't want to get involved with her, Tilly. I know you're missing Josephine but you must try to make some decent friends.'

'Kate Oswald isn't my friend!' Tilly blurted angrily, standing up. 'She hates me!'

'Hate is a strong word,' Ivy told her gently.

'Yeah, well, I hate her too!' Tilly felt tears gathering behind her eyes. Thanks to Kate, she had ruined family dinner. Her home was supposed to be a haven from the stresses of school but somehow they had followed her in like a persistent shadow and darkened the dining table.

'That's it.' Clive smacked his palms against the table, which shook beneath him, the tape which held it together underneath now struggling.

'Tilly, you got a detention and it's no one's fault but your own. You're grounded for the rest of the week.'

'Dad, that's hardly a punishment!' Maria objected, pointing at her little sister. 'She stays in her room all the time!'

'It's the punishment we give you girls for a detention so it's the same for Tilly,' Clive told them.

'Well, it's not fair.' Maria was folding her arms over her chest, a dark scowl hardening her features.

'Life isn't fair,' their father said softly. His rage seemed to be suddenly ebbing out of him, filtering silently into the air.

'You heard your father.' Ivy reached for Tilly's hand and gave it a squeeze. 'You're grounded for the rest of this week.'

Tilly nodded before turning and running out of the room. She heard her father shout after her that she needed to finish her dinner but she'd already lost her appetite.

There was mutiny amongst the townspeople. Tilly could hear their angry cries as she was led to the safety of her tower. The air carried the scent of distant fires somewhere in the distance. Coughing, Tilly allowed her guards to lead her deeper in to the forest, away from the agitated crowds.

'There is unrest among the people,' her head guard told her, his tone hard.

'I know,' Tilly nodded at him. 'But what we can do?'

'There's nothing you can do, your Majesty. This summer has been long and hard and the land is the land dry and barren. Once the rains come the crops will be replenished and peace will be restored.'

'Until then?'

'Until then you must remain in your tower where it is safe. The rains should arrive by the end of the week. Your people will settle.'

Tilly let him boost her up towards the tower. Carefully, she climbed the familiar route amongst the ornate brick work and vines. With each step the roar of the crowds became more distant. Soon it was nothing more than a whisper upon the wind.

Alone, Tilly gave a soft sigh of relief. She had missed the sweeping stone floor and stained glass windows which offered a breath-taking view of her Kingdom. Everything was how she had left it, right down to her book still resting beside the fireplace open on the page she had last read. The fire was now merely embers in the hearth but Tilly didn't mind. The arduous climb had left her flushed and warm. She picked up her book and moved towards her four poster bed which was covered in soft furs and sumptuous silk sheets. Nuzzling against the fabrics, Tilly felt a million miles away from her problems. She drew her book close and began to read the next chapter.

She read until her eyes strained against the growing darkness as day began to blur into night. Outside, she could hear crickets chirping, replacing the soft bird song which had lazily carried on the breeze. Tilly was safe in her tower. Sighing contentedly, she let her eyes flutter and close.

'Tilly!'

Eyes flying open, Tilly sat up too quickly, making her head swim. She squinted against the sudden brightness as the overhead light was flicked on.

'Tilly.' Her mother looked up at the tower. 'Here.' She was carefully holding a plate of half-eaten dinner in one hand, which shook slightly, causing the cutlery to jingle together like seasonal bells.

'You need to finish your dinner, sweetheart.'

'But you're mad at me,' Tilly pouted before rolling over and facing the wall.

'I am mad,' her mother said. 'But only because I expect better from you. You've always been such a good girl, Tilly. I don't want you to start getting detentions and do badly in school.'

'Why not?' Tilly objected. 'Monica and Maria get detentions all the time.'

'You're different.' Tilly felt a hand softly stroke her back. 'You've always been more sensitive than they are. I don't want you to lose that.'

Tilly heard the crack in her mother's voice, which made her decide to turn over. Ivy smiled warmly at her and offered the plate of dinner, her hand still shaking.

'You need to finish your dinner so you grow up big and strong.'

'I'll never be big and strong,' Tilly objected, but she sat up and swung her legs over the side of her bed anyway.

'Mum, you're shaking,' she noted.

'So I am.' Ivy looked at her hand in surprise.

'I'm sorry you're finding school difficult,' her mother said. 'Sometimes life challenges us in ways we don't understand,' Ivy added, wringing her hands together as if trying to work the shakes out of them.

'Like when we went to Cornwall and you and Dad only brought one tape?' Tilly asked as she shoved a forkful of gravy-soaked chicken in to her mouth.

'Yes,' her mother laughed, the sound as soft and magical as dainty silver bells. 'Just like that.'

And So She Slept for a Thousand Years

Tilly's sisters were right: being trapped up in her bedroom was hardly a punishment. After she'd finished eating, Tilly carefully came down from her tower and positioned herself on her lower bunk bed.

She glanced longingly at her pile of DVDs, at the latest edition where the blue glitter of the princess' dress sparkled on the cover. Tilly reached for it and tilted it towards the light. This was another of her favourite films. In the movie the princess wasn't animated, she was very much real with long, golden hair and a dashing prince. Tilly traced a finger over the dress. She yearned to watch it, to get lost in the storyline and have her heart freeze at the crucial moment when all might be ruined by a wicked stepmother. But that would require going downstairs and she was banished to her room, just like the princess in the film who was sent up to the attic where she had only mice for company.

Her little television was still lacking a DVD player so Tilly had to content herself with watching whatever was on the regular channels. She pressed the power button and the screen illuminated after several seconds. There was a property show on where a young-looking couple were being shown around apartments. Tilly huddled against one of her pillows and settled down, imagining the couple were actually royalty forced to go incognito. Tilly giggled to herself as she interpreted their tense facial expressions for fear that their cover was about to be blown.

Despite the game she attached to it, the property show failed to hold her attention for longer than twenty minutes. Tilly sat up, feeling restless. Her DVD sparkled from where she had left it on the duvet cover. It was pleading with her to at least just watch the beginning. Tilly chewed her lip and considered what her family might be doing.

Her father would be reading the newspaper in

the kitchen like he always did after dinner. Monica and Maria would be in their room arguing over what to listen to on their CD player while they pretended to do their homework. Tilly's mother would be cleaning up dinner or pruning the rose bushes in their tiny garden. No one would be using the television until at least nine o'clock.

Tilly sent a desperate look towards her pink princess clock on the wall beside her window. It was only half past seven. Committing to her decision, Tilly grabbed her DVD and cautiously crept towards the door. She held her breath as she opened it, waiting for someone to pounce from the other side and tell her to remain in her room. But no one appeared – the small, carpeted landing was empty. Taking a deep breath, Tilly darted out and slid down the staircase, making sure to avoid the step near the bottom which always creaked.

The living room was empty. Soon, her parents would come to occupy the threadbare sofa, snuggling up to watch a detective show on TV. But for now Tilly was alone. She was almost bubbling over with excitement as she hurried over to the DVD player. She could already hear the opening music to her beloved film

Feeling deliciously mischievous, she started the film, sitting cross-legged in front the screen and gazing up at it.

Tilly loved the world in the movie where the fields were full of wild flowers which crept up on to the heroine's dress. Tilly became absorbed by the film. The characters pulled her in to their perfect world, making their pain hers. Tilly could scarcely breathe when the heroine's mother took ill. Especially because she knew what was coming. Each time the little girl lost her mother, Tilly felt as though she'd been delivered a blow which knocked the air right out of her lungs. It was so awful, so unimaginable, so –

'Tilly!'

She straightened and fumbled for the remote, which was precariously held together with black tape. Pausing the film, Tilly turned around, her face burning with shame.

'You know you shouldn't be down here.' Her mother was doing her best to sound angry. Her hair was damp around her shoulders which emphasised how thin it had become in recent months. Her cheeks were glossed with a soft glow. Had she just been having a shower?

'Mum, I'm sorry, I just …' Tilly glanced back helplessly at the frozen image on the screen.

'You were told to stay in your room.'

'I know.'

'You're grounded, remember?'

'I know.' Tilly hung her head. She'd disappointed her mother again. 'I just wanted to watch my film. Not all of it, just a little bit. I swear I wasn't going to stay here long, it's just that I don't have a DVD player in my room.' She was talking too quickly, her words tumbling against one another. She hoped that she could somehow avert her mother's anger with her voice alone.

'Tilly, that's the point of a punishment,' Ivy sighed, 'you have to go without something you want.'

Tilly reached for the DVD case within her grasp. What was so wrong with wanting to watch a movie? Especially when no one else was using the television?

'You can watch it another time,' her mother was saying, indicating with her eyes that it was time for Tilly to head back upstairs.

'OK.' Tilly gave a stubborn sigh before ejecting her disc and returning it to its glittering case.

'You've already seen that one a dozen times.'

'What difference does that make?' Tilly wondered.

'Don't you get … bored?'

'Bored?' Tilly repeated the word as though she didn't understand its meaning.

'Yes, Tilly, bored. You watch the same things over and over. Not like your sisters, their tastes change on a weekly basis.'

'But I like my movies.' Tilly was clutching her DVD to her chest.

'I know, sweetheart.' Ivy smiled softly at her. 'But there are thousands of movies. Don't you ever think about the ones you might be missing out on?'

'No.'

'OK. Well, upstairs. And you stay in your bedroom this time, got it?'

'Yeah,' Tilly gave a slow nod. 'I got it.'

By nine o'clock it was dark, and Tilly was wearing her long, blue nightgown which had the princess in her sparkling dress decorating the front of it. When she wore the nightgown Tilly liked to pretend she was actually wearing the glittering dress. Tilly's hair was gathered down her back in one long plait and her mouth tingled from the mint of the toothpaste she'd just used. This was when she was supposed to go to bed.

Beyond her bedroom door she could hear her sisters starting up their usual evening routine of annoying their father by either playing their music too loudly or taking too long in the bathroom.

'I don't know what they do in there!' he'd complain to their mother. 'They spend hours in there, and then when I go in there's steam everywhere, shaving foam all over the tiles, and wet towels on the floor!'

'They're teenage girls,' Ivy would tell him lightly with a dismissive wave of her hand.

'They're monsters,' Clive would mutter to himself.

Tilly was leaning against her door, taking comfort in the familiar discussions occurring out on the landing.

'Dad! It's not too loud!' Monica shouted defiantly down the stairs.

'I can barely hear the TV!' their father shouted back.

'Then turn it up!'

'Monica, don't make me come up there!'

He always threatened to come up there, but he never did. He wouldn't dare risk missing a moment of his beloved shows.

'Think about your mother!'

Doors slammed dramatically but the hum of music drifting from the other side of the house grew softer. Smiling, Tilly climbed back up her tower.

Tilly awoke to voices just outside her door. Rolling over in the darkness, she drew her duvet up against her chin. For a moment the dream she was in filtered out into the room and she wondered if the people outside were there to kidnap her, that they had been sent by the townspeople. Tilly hoped that if she remained perfectly still and silent that they might leave.

'I'm worried about her.' She recognised the weary lilt of her mother's voice. It was her parents outside her door. She was safe and at home; no one was coming to take her away.

'She just needs to grow up,' her father stated.

'That's easier said than done.'

'She's at secondary school. She'll have to grow up soon, even if she doesn't want to.'

'I just … I don't want her to change.'

'She won't.'

'She will, Clive.' Her mother's voice hardened. 'She's so innocent, and that's going to be taken away from her and I worry she's not … equipped for things.'

'Is anyone ever properly equipped? Some days I struggle to cope, let alone the girls.'

'She wraps herself up in these fairy tales and it's like living in a giant ball of cotton wool. She's detached from the world, Clive, and I think that's dangerous.'

'You're over thinking it.'

'Am I?'

Tilly quickly snapped her eyes closed as her bedroom door opened. She heard her mother gently walk over to the bed and lean up towards the top bunk.

'Night-night, princess,' her mother whispered, her breath was warm as she drew close and kissed Tilly's cheek. 'Sleep tight.'

A tear fell where the kiss had been planted as

her mother closed the door. Tilly tightened into a ball and tried to dismiss what she had heard. Tears dripped onto her pillow as she shivered beneath her duvet. Why would her mother call her a princess if she really thought Tilly needed to grow up? Didn't her mother like her anymore? Tilly thought of the times they had sat together watching films and eating biscuits and drinking lemonade. Those were some of her happiest memories but her mother obviously didn't feel the same. Betrayal burned through Tilly as she continued to cry. Her shoulders shook and her body trembled but she took care not to make a sound. She didn't want to draw her mother's attention.

At breakfast, Tilly had no appetite. She pushed her cereal around in her bowl but ate hardly any. The conversation she'd overheard the night before haunted her, but more than that she feared the day ahead: the day when she'd spend a lunchtime detention with Kate Oswald. The prospect was terrifying.

'Tilly, eat your breakfast,' her father told her. Lately he was the one who prepared breakfast, which meant they only ever had cereal and juice. When her mother used to get up with them she would make porridge or scrambled eggs and serve tea. But lately, her mother was always sleeping in. Tilly resented that she was now too lazy to see her off to school.

'I'm not hungry.' Tilly dropped her spoon into her bowl and pushed it away.

'You've got to eat something,' her dad sighed.

'Is your detention today?' Maria asked as she appeared in the kitchen, running her hands through her long hair.

'Yeah.'

'Ooh, have fun,' she laughed.

'Maria, come and eat.' Clive pointed at the table and the empty bowls which were surrounded by several tall boxes of cereal.

'Dad, I don't do breakfast,' she told him with a hair flick. 'You know that.'

The sound of footsteps upon the staircase proceeded Monica's arrival in to the kitchen. Her hair was gathered on top of her head in a messy bun which made her cheekbones appear even more pronounced than usual. Tilly slid down in her chair. She wished she was as beautiful as her sisters but she doubted she'd ever be willing to dedicate as much time as they did on her appearance. Her sisters were always preening: plucking this, waxing that, straightening something else. Maintaining their looks seemed like a never-ending task.

'Monica, breakfast.' Clive ordered, raising his voice.

Laughing, Monica shook her head, 'Yeah, right.'

'Are you ready?' Maria addressed Monica. They took a moment to check each other's makeup before giving nods. They were about to head through the door when Maria paused, glancing back at Tilly.

'Squirt has detention today.' She raised a hand towards the table.

'Really?' Monica seemed instantly amused. 'Have fun.'

'It's detention, not a disco!' their father said, his nostrils flaring.

'Careful, Dad, next she'll be getting a tattoo!' Monica giggled.

'Do you have a tattoo?' Clive was staring at his daughter in horror.

Maria was laughing heartily as she leaned against her sister.

'Come on, we need to go.' They were giggling as they headed out the door.

'See, this is why you should eat breakfast.' Tilly's father wilted in his chair and pushed the bowl back towards her. 'I refuse to have another of my daughters turn into one of those.'

'One of what?' Tilly asked as she reluctantly picked up her spoon and continued nudging around the cereal.

'A teenager.'

'I think that's inevitable, Dad,' Tilly told him as she forced down a mouthful of cereal. She frowned as she chewed. Wasn't that what everyone wanted, for her to grow up and become like her sisters? Her head was starting to throb from the mixed messages she was receiving.

'Is your detention today?'

Tilly nodded.

'Well, take the time to think about why you're there and make sure it never happens again, OK?'

Tilly nodded.

'You don't think your sister really has a tattoo, do you?'

Tilly remained silent.

Kate ignored Tilly during registration, which she considered to be a blessing. Perhaps she was so mad about the detention she'd been rendered speechless. Tilly hoped the effect would last the rest of the school year. But when lunchtime arrived and Tilly trudged over to Miss Havishorn's classroom she found Kate leaning against the doorframe and her power of speech had returned.

'Thanks for this,' she said sarcastically as Tilly stood beside her.

'It wasn't my fault.'

'Please,' Kate scoffed, and she exhaled sharply, blowing away blonde strands of hair which had gathered in front of her eyes.

'Where are Sophie and Claire?' Tilly noticed that Kate was alone, a phenomenon that hadn't happened in years. Usually, wherever Kate went her loyal posse followed.

'They didn't get detention, did they?' Kate said with a tightness in her voice.

'No,' Tilly admitted, 'they didn't.'

'I mean, they could have come along for support but no. They'd rather go off to the field and watch the guys play football.'

Tilly couldn't think of a duller way to spend her lunch hour. In her free time she liked to visit the library and discover new books, but she had a tendency to be drawn to books she already loved, eager to read them over and over. Maybe her mother was right; maybe she was missing out on things because she kept seeking out the same experiences.

'Were your parents mad?' Tilly wondered, remembering the disappointment etched into her mother's features.

'About what?'

'About the detention.' Tilly tried not to sound too shocked. What else was there to be mad about?

'They don't know.'

'They don't know?'

'For them to know, Terry would have to acknowledge my existence.'

'Who's Terry?'

'My dad,' Kate replied flatly.

'Doesn't he work with my dad?'

'Probably,' Kate shrugged. 'I don't know. We're not close.'

Tilly was about to say something when Miss

Havishorn's imposing figure loomed over them.

'Come on,' she said briskly as she unlocked her classroom door. 'Let's get this over with. You're not the only ones giving up your lunch time.'

The girls were told to sit on separate desks and write about why they shouldn't talk during registration.

'At least one hundred words,' Miss Havishorn insisted, which caused Kate to roll her eyes dramatically. 'Miss Oswald, I can assure you that I'll be counting every word.'

'I'm sure you will,' Kate replied in a sickly sweet tone.

Tilly opened up a crisp new page in her notebook and began to think over the task at hand but her mind quickly began to wander. She thought about what Kate had said about her father, about how they weren't close. What if he were some tyrant who tormented not only his daughter but Tilly's father, the King? Terry Oswald might be behind the uprising amongst the people.

He might be out there holding court, declaring it was time the people climbed up the stone tower and stole the princess held inside. Tilly shuddered. She wished she had a fairy godmother who could intervene.

A quick glance around the classroom made Tilly yearn to see the desks turned into ornate wooden sledges, the whiteboard to a slick wall of ice which would turn the entire school into a giant snow castle. Tilly's drab uniform would transform into a glittering blue gown and her fairy godmother would place her in one of the sledges and turn Kate into a snow-white unicorn. The unicorn would pull the sledge across the slick floors, out of the ice castle, and into the world, away from Terry Oswald and his quest to overthrow the Kingdom.

'Tick tock, Miss Johnson.'

The ice melted in an instant and Tilly was back with Miss Havishorn glaring angrily at her. Tilly pressed her mermaid pen against the page and began to write.

After twenty minutes, Miss Havishorn shifted in her chair and pushed her glasses up her nose.

'OK, what do you have?'

'Miss Havishorn, we already know why we shouldn't talk during registration, we don't need to write a hundred words about it.' Kate stubbornly crossed her arms. Glancing over,

Tilly could see her piece of paper was still blank.

'So why shouldn't you?'

'Because you say so.'

Miss Havishorn's eyes widened with displeasure.

'Because I say so?' she repeated, rising to her feet. 'Is that an adequate response, Matilda?'

Miss Havishorn's head swivelled on her thick neck to look at Tilly, who was cringing upon hearing her full name.

'It's disrespectful to talk during registration,' Tilly said meekly. 'So we should be quiet and listen.'

'Do you think you could accomplish that in future?' Miss Havishorn was looking between them.

'Yes,' Tilly blurted desperately. 'Of course.'

'Sure,' Kate shrugged.

'OK then.' Miss Havishorn nodded with satisfaction. 'Go and enjoy the rest of your lunch break.'

Tilly began to pack away her things. Kate hadn't done the task they had been set, how could they be dismissed?

Tilly had to hurry to catch up with Kate, who'd left with such urgency you'd think the classroom was on fire.

'Hey,' Tilly called. Kate spun around, her lips curling up in annoyance.

'Yes?' she demanded.

'You didn't do the task. Why not?'

'Because it was stupid,' Kate declared.

'But we still had to do it.'

'No, we didn't,' Kate insisted, rolling her eyes, which drew Tilly's attention to Kate's poorly applied eyeliner. 'Miss Havishorn was on a power trip. She just wanted to make sure we wouldn't talk in registration again, and guess what, we won't! Lesson learned.'

'How did you know she wouldn't check our work?'

'I didn't.'

'But you still didn't do it?'

'Jeez, you're so uptight!' Kate glanced along the corridor, blatantly eager to get away from Tilly. 'What's the worst that could happen? She gives me another detention?'

'That doesn't worry you?' Tilly couldn't understand how Kate could be so flippant. She had the same attitude as Monica and Maria but was a few years below them – had they been as blasé as Kate?

'No, it doesn't worry me,' Kate said tersely, her tone almost scolding. 'I worry about who I'll sit with at lunch or what I'm doing Saturday. I don't waste energy worrying about detentions. And neither should you. You're such a little princess.'

Kate stalked off, taking her sweet aroma with her. Tilly stared after her in confusion. Why would anyone worry about what they were doing Saturday? They were one of the best days of the week. Tilly would be allowed to have a big bowl of popcorn as watched one of her DVDs in the lounge. Then she'd go to bed and read until her eyes ached. How did worrying about things like detentions make her a princess?

'So, you survived?'

The dinner hall was almost empty, as Tilly was late. Everyone else was outside enjoying the rare sunshine warming the trimmed grass in the playing field. Tilly put down her cheese sandwich and looked up to see Maria, one hand loosely placed on her hip.

'I told Mum I'd check in on you,' she explained as she dropped down on the bench.

'I survived,' Tilly nodded.

'Good.' Maria smiled though it didn't reach her eyes. 'Just think of it as a rite of passage.'

Her sister was preparing to leave but Tilly wanted her there a few moments longer. Lunch times felt unbearably long when she ate alone.

'Did you used to worry about getting detention?'

'Huh?' Maria frowned as she lingered beside the table. 'I guess when I was in your year.'

'What made you stop worrying about it?'

Maria shrugged. Tilly noticed how her sister's dark hair glimmered in the sunlight. If only she had the same locks. Instead, her hair was the colour of dirt and dry leaves. It didn't shimmer in sunlight or sway elegantly with her every movement. Tilly's hair tumbled in confused curls which didn't seem to know which way was down.

'Tilly.' Maria chewed her lip. 'Try not to worry about detentions, OK? I know Mum and Dad make out like they're a big deal but there are bigger things to worry about.'

'Like what?' Tilly blinked innocently.

'Like …' Maria nervously twirled a dark strand of hair around her finger.

'Like a meteor crashing into Earth and killing everyone?' Tilly recalled a film she'd once caught. It had terrified her to her core.

'Yes,' Maria pointed towards Tilly. 'Big stuff like that.'

'OK.' Tilly was left slightly confused.

'But you're OK? – About detention and stuff?' Maria was sending longing looks to the double doors which led outside.

'Yeah,' Tilly nodded as she raised her sandwich to her mouth. 'I'm OK.'

Two Ugly Step-sisters

Tilly was getting better at disappearing once she got to school. She allowed herself to get absorbed by the swarm of students and she drifted absently through her days. She no longer felt like a salmon struggling up stream. Instead, she let herself get carried along with the flow.

Tilly knew better than to get complacent. It was only her third week and the map she'd been given seemed just as confusing as it had on her first day. Normally, she'd follow a familiar face to her next class after eavesdropping on where they were headed.

Tilly did her best to focus when the bell would ring. Then she would pack away her things swiftly, and hurry out with everyone else.

'Those who fail to prepare should prepare to

fail,' her mother would advise. Tilly was prepared. She was managing to navigate around the concrete maze and she was achieving her goal – she was surviving.

It was a Friday morning, which meant that everyone was in high spirits.

'We're going to the cinema tonight,' Kate gushed to her sidekicks.

'My dad said he can give us a lift,' Claire gloated.

'How nice of him to take an evening off from being bitter and divorced,' Kate chimed in. Claire grew red and opened her mouth, but Sophie interrupted.

'I heard Michael Daniels is going to watch the new Transformers film.'

'Then it's settled, we'll see that,' Kate declared.

'Really?' Claire whined. 'I don't like those movies.'

'Whether or not you like them doesn't matter,' Kate told her sternly. 'What matters is that guys like them and will be there. Got it?'

'Got it,' Claire mumbled.

'You should be grateful you've got plans on a Friday night,' Kate told her, 'you could be stuck home like Matilda, and wouldn't that be tragic?'

Tilly vaguely heard the insult, but didn't react. She was too wrapped up in her own thoughts to care.

On a Friday, Tilly had Geography followed by French. Her first class had finished and she was heading towards the language block but she'd slipped up. When her Geography teacher, Mr Stanton, had started discussing far off continents, Tilly's mind had begun to drift. She imagined distant lands with vast mountain ranges, the tips of which looked like they'd been sprinkled with icing sugar.

In these lands, the people were rugged and wore thick furs to ward off the harsh, cold winters. In their weather-beaten homes they would crowd around fires to warm their frost-bitten fingers. But against this unforgiving backdrop a hero would emerge – a princess who could tame the weather. With one flick of her wrist she could bring the sun. Some thought she was a witch. She had golden hair infused with light and her skin was radiant. She was the princess the inhabitants of the icy land had been waiting for, yearning for...

The bell screamed through Tilly's thoughts,

evaporating the winter world to mere vapours.

'Focus, Tilly,' she berated herself as she began to quickly shove her notebook and pencil case into her backpack. Around her, desks were already emptying. 'You should always focus,' she reminded herself under her breath as she pulled on her backpack and hurried out of the door. Even though there were no familiar faces in sight, Tilly was confident she knew the way to the language block. She darted down the nearest flight of stairs and crossed the yard.

The wind had grown sharp and scratched against Tilly's cheeks as she hurried to the other side of the building. She scurried up two more flights of stairs and reached the language block – only it wasn't. She was in the science building. She was suddenly skewered by despair, lost and running out of time. Soon, a second bell would sound, the one that meant all students should be in their seat. If Tilly was late she risked another detention. The thought made her dizzy.

She stood on the spot and tried to imagine the school map tucked away at the bottom of her backpack. She didn't have time to reach for it. She tried to think where was the science building in relation to the language block, tried to see the route but the princess of the sun was lingering on the edge of her thoughts, demanding attention.

'Come on.' Tilly pressed a hand anxiously to her temple. She could do this.

The blue double doors ahead of her opened and a group of girls headed her way. They walked with their heads held high. A sweet-smelling cloud quickly reached Tilly's senses. She was about to turn away from the girls when she spotted Maria walking in the centre with a pretty blonde and a stern-faced brunette.

'Maria.' Tilly tumbled over towards her sister, her face lighting up with hope. 'Oh, thank goodness. I'm lost. How do I get to the language block?'

The blonde snickered. The gesture reminded Tilly of Kate.

'Please,' Tilly insisted, gazing up at her sister's eyes, which were framed by too much eyeliner.

'Oh dear, are you lost?' the brunette mocked. She wore an unflattering shade of purple lipstick which made her cheeks seem deathly pale.

'Maria,' Tilly addressed her sister. 'Please help me out.'

'Is that your sister?' the blonde asked, as a

long-nailed hand fluttered up to her chest. 'Oh my God, she's a geek.'

Tilly couldn't tell if Maria was blushing. The concealer she eagerly applied to her face each morning meant she was always the same orange-tinted shade of beige.

'Just point me in the right direction,' Tilly pleaded. 'I'm going to be late.'

'Oh no, and the world will end!' the brunette said with an overly dramatic gasp.

'Why are you being mean?' Tilly finally looked away from Maria. She instantly felt the sting of the cruel gaze her sister's friends regarded her with.

'Get lost, squirt.'

Tilly recoiled and looked at her sister in stunned surprise.

'You heard me, get lost,' Maria repeated.

Shaken, Tilly moved aside so her sister and her friends could stroll past. She could hear them laughing as they moved further down the corridor. Tilly leaned against the wall, feeling like she'd been pierced by an arrow to the chest. Why had Maria been so nasty? Why hadn't she defended her? Why was everyone at Dullerton Secondary School so impossibly mean? With a trembling hand, she had no choice but to search for her map at the bottom of her backpack. She was going to be late; there was no escaping that now.

'Bonjour, Mademoiselle Johnson!' the slim French teacher exclaimed as Tilly skulked in through the door. She sensed the rest of the class swivel in her direction but she didn't look at them.

'Why are you late to my class?' the teacher demanded, her words still holding a trace of her French accent.

'I got lost,' Tilly admitted. It was the truth, after all. She expected her teacher to laugh at her, taunt her for being so stupid. Instead, she waved a hand in Tilly's direction, indicating for her to sit down.

'It's a big school,' the teacher noted. 'It takes some getting used to.'

Tilly sagged with relief. She'd been certain that she would receive another detention. She was so thankful not to be in trouble that she almost forgot about her unpleasant interaction with Maria.

'So next week you're going to start walking to school, is that OK?' Tilly's dad asked.

'Yeah,' Tilly nodded as she gazed out of the window. 'That's fine.'

'I'm going to be on a different shift next month.'

'It's OK.'

'I got something today that I think you'll be excited about.'

'Oh?' Tilly shifted to look across at her father. He was smiling from behind the wheel. He hardly ever smiled to the point that when he did, it didn't seem to suit him.

'A guy at work was selling his old one off cheap,' her father explained, still wearing an unfamiliar grin.

'His old what?'

'Computer.'

'A computer?' Tilly was smiling too. Computers were in schools, libraries, and other people's homes. But now they had one! It meant she could actually type out her homework instead of writing everything out by hand.

'Yep' Her father's smile widened to reveal

teeth which were always slightly yellow due to years of chain smoking. 'You girls have been begging me for one for ages! Well, your sisters have. Don't get too excited. It's an old model so it's not that great, but I figured we'd be able to use it just the same.'

'Dad that's ... that's awesome!' Tilly gushed.

'Yeah,' he was nodding in satisfaction. 'I thought you'd be pleased.'

That evening, the computer received its grand unveiling. The family gathered in the dining room and stood around the table where a portion was concealed beneath a faded gingham cloth.

'You can't keep it here,' Ivy told her husband sternly.

'It's just for the time being,' Clive explained. Tilly could see the bulk beneath the table cloth and the dark cables which led from it towards the socket in the wall.

'Yeah, Dad, we want it in our room,' Monica said.

'Yeah!' Maria agreed. 'It should be in our room.'

'No!' Clive snapped. 'This computer is for everybody. Besides, I don't want you sat up there in your room on face chat all the time.'

'Facebook,' Maria corrected.

'The computer is primarily for homework.' Clive was gesturing towards the bulge beneath the fabric, relishing his moment as ring master.

'Well, can we at least see it?' Ivy pressed him.

With a dramatic flourish, Tilly's father pulled back the table cloth, revealing the aged machine.

'What do you think?' he asked his family.

Tilly looked at the computer, which did seem to be an older model than the ones she used at school. The base unit was on the floor and already omitting a low hum. On the table stood the large monitor and a keyboard where some of the keys had fallen off. But still, it was a computer.

'Daddy, it's great!' Tilly clapped her hands excitedly.

'Thanks, princess.'

'Dad, it sucks,' Monica pouted. 'It's so old. Does it even get the internet? What's the download speed like?'

'It's all set up,' her father told her proudly, 'and password protected,' he quickly added. 'So don't think you can go looking up anything inappropriate.'

Monica rolled her eyes and sighed.

'Dad, we're girls, we're not going to jerk off to porn on it!' Maria declared fiercely.

'Language!' Ivy snapped, casting a protective glance in Tilly's direction.

'She hears far worse at school, trust me,' Monica stated.

'You might want to show your dad a bit of gratitude,' Ivy told her daughters, tentatively reaching for one of the chairs to lean against as though she were at risk of losing her balance.

'This was an expensive investment for this family and he was thinking of you when he bought it.'

Monica was already walking out of the room but she turned briefly.

'It's a guilt gift, Mum, and you know why. You think buying this makes what's happening OK?'

Tilly looked between her sisters, about to ask what a guilt gift was when Maria spoke up -

'Thanks, Dad.' but her words sounded forced.

Monica scowled before disappearing through the door.

'At least someone's excited.' Clive tenderly placed a hand on Tilly's shoulder. 'Want to have a go?'

Tilly bounced up and down on the spot.

'Yes please!'

'I'm going first,' Maria interrupted, placing herself down on the chair in front of it. 'I've got homework to do,' she explained with a sickly smile.

Tilly felt the air leave her lungs like a deflated balloon.

'You can have a go later,' her mother said softly, still leaning against the chair. 'For now, why don't you go and watch a DVD in the front room?'

'I'm not grounded anymore?' Tilly wondered warily.

'No,' Ivy smiled. 'You're not grounded anymore.'

'Yes!' Tilly bounded out of the room and sprinted up the stairs. She couldn't wait to watch her movie.

The smell of dinner travelled through the house. They would be having lasagne. Tilly's belly rumbled as she sat in front of the television, her head gazing in adoration at the film that was playing.

She was singing along with the inhabitants of the castle, who were welcoming their newest guest. The rumbles in Tilly's tummy grew louder as she sung about the different delicious kinds of food. She was so preoccupied with the film that she didn't hear the door from the dining room open.

'Hey,' Maria called out to her.

Tilly turned in surprise.

'Sorry, was I being loud?' She fumbled for the remote and lowered the volume on the television.

'No.' Maria shook her head. Most of her eyeliner had been rubbed away during the day so she looked fresh-faced. In the doorway, backlit by the dining room lights, she looked her age. There was only a year's difference between Maria and Monica, which accounted for them being so close. Monica was fifteen and would celebrate her sixteenth birthday before the end of the year.

'Come here, I want to show you something.' Maria nodded towards the dining room. Tilly paused her movie and untangled her legs so she could follow her sister into the other room.

'OK, sit down,' Maria ordered, pointing at the chair in front of the computer. Tilly glanced at her but didn't move.

'Seriously, sit down. It's all right.'

Silently, Tilly sat down. The computer was humming loudly like a rocket ship preparing to launch. Was that it? Maria had programmed it to go to the moon and take Tilly with it?

'Right, look here.' Maria came behind her to use the mouse. She clicked on a few icons and the screen became blue.

'This is Skype,' Maria explained. 'I downloaded it.'

'What does it do?'

'It lets you chat to people who are far away. People like Josephine.'

Tilly blinked and pushed back her chair. She spun around to look at her sister.

'Why would you want to help me chat to Josephine?'

Maria's mouth drooped as she looked towards

the kitchen where their mother was preparing dinner.

'I'm just trying to do you a solid,' she shrugged. 'I was a jerk earlier. I should have helped you out.'

'Why didn't you?'

'Because …' Maria pushed a hand through her dark hair. 'Because you don't make it easy, Tilly. It's like you're dead set on not fitting in.'

Tilly's eyes remained scrutinising.

'Most people, all they want is to fit in.' Maria crouched so they were at the same level. 'They listen to the music everyone else likes, cut their hair in whatever style is fashionable. But you – you don't care about that crap. You like what you like.'

'What's wrong with that?'

'Nothing.' Maria sighed and bit her lip. 'It's just … that's not the way to be popular. It's not the way to make friends. At school, it's better to be part of the herd. Am I making sense?'

'Like a sheep?'

'Kind of, yeah.'

'But I don't want to be a sheep.'

'I know, Tilly, I know. Look, maybe I'm not explaining myself very well. I'm sorry about today. I hope being able to talk with Josephine will make up for it. I know school has been tough. We're just ... we're all going through some stuff right now.'

'Are you a sheep?' Tilly blinked at her sister.

'Argh, see I didn't explain myself very well. I'm not ... well ... maybe.' Maria coughed and stood up. 'I don't make waves, Tilly, I put my head down and fit in. That way I don't end up alone on a Saturday night.'

Tilly looked away, back towards the blue screen of the computer. What was so important about having plans on a Saturday night? It made no sense.

'So, if you want to talk to Josephine you click here.' Maria moved the mouse to the relevant button. 'And if she's online then boom! You're talking.'

Tilly eyed the screen uneasily. It was difficult to believe that with the click of a button she could be looking at her best friend who felt a million miles away.

'Thank you.'

'It's no problem, just ... I'm going to be there for you more.' Maria gave her shoulder a squeeze before leaving the room.

Tilly had to wait until after dinner to Skype Josephine. As everyone ate their lasagne her father interrogated Maria about what the programme actually was.

'How do you know Tilly won't be chatting to anyone?' he demanded.

'It doesn't work like that, Dad,' Maria assured him.

'I mean, she might start being … what is it? "Made over"?'

Monica snorted.

'Dad.' Maria fought the urge to laugh. 'You mean groomed. And anyway, Skype isn't like that. You know who you're talking to.'

'Oh.' Clive didn't sound convinced.

'I'll sit and do some sewing while they chat,' Mum offered helpfully.

'Thanks.' Tilly smiled but noticed that most of her dinner was still untouched.

'Aren't you hungry, Mum?'

Ivy blushed as she looked down at her plate. She caught her husband's steely gaze and shook her head.

'I'm just feeling a bit sick. It'll pass.'

'OK,' Tilly said brightly as she finished off her lasagne.

It was almost eight o'clock when Josephine finally came online. This surprised Tilly as she knew her friend had her own laptop as well as an iPad. It felt surreal to have the computer ring out as though it were a telephone. At the other end of the table Tilly's mother sat quietly, darning a few pairs of socks and pretending not to listen.

After several rings the blue screen was replaced by a close up of Josephine. Tilly felt her stomach twist in bittersweet joy.

'Hi!' Tilly waved enthusiastically at the black orb attached to the top of the screen which served as her webcam. Maria had advised her to talk directly into it instead of at the screen.

'Tilly, hi!' Josephine gushed.

'I've missed you so much!' Tilly told her.

'Aw, I've missed you too.'

Tilly was smiling so much her cheeks were starting to ache but then she noticed something different about Josephine. At first she thought it

108

was just the computer but now she was certain something had changed.

'What happened to your hair?'

'Oh, do you like it?' Josephine was smiling, revealing the little dimples in her cheeks as she pulled on a strand of her long, dark hair. Previously she'd had such tight curls that she looked part poodle. But now all her hair was smooth and straight, like how Monica and Maria wore theirs.

'Did you straighten it?' Tilly wondered.

'Yeah.' Josephine ran her hands over her sleek mane, revealing sparkling nails.

'You've painted your nails!'

'Yeah.' Josephine held her manicure towards her laptop's camera, offering Tilly a prime view of her glitter nail polish.

'Everyone at my school wears nail polish,' she shrugged.

'Oh.'

'So how do you like school?' Josephine was still smiling.

Tilly wanted to be honest, to say how much she hated school and yearned for a release from her five-year sentence. But from the corner of her eye she could make out her mother, sat with her head bent and threading a needle. It was difficult to tell if her expression was pinched from concern or concentration. Either way, Tilly didn't want to risk worrying her.

'It's OK. I'm still kind of finding my way around. What about you?'

'I love my school!' Josephine declared giddily. 'All the girls are so nice and they live near me. Tomorrow, a group of us are going to the cinema.'

'Tomorrow?' That would be Saturday night, the infamous evening when you were supposedly cursed if you didn't go out.

'Uh-huh.' Josephine was nodding eagerly. 'You'll have to come down and meet everyone! There's Poppy and Lilac, oh and Vivian. We could have a sleepover.'

'They've all been nice to you?'

'So nice!' Josephine looked like she'd never stop smiling. 'And there's so much to do, Tilly! Yesterday I saw Lily James crossing the street, can you believe it?'

Tilly gazed blankly at her friend.

'Lily James!' Josephine repeated, her tone urgent and excited. Tilly could only shake her head.

'Jeez, Tilly, she's Cinderella in the new movie. I thought that was like, one of your favourite films!'

Suddenly, Tilly felt like she was talking with one of her sisters. Cinderella wasn't one of her favourite films it was one of theirs. Josephine seemed to have forgotten that.

'How did she look?' Tilly enquired politely.

'Stunning!' Josephine responded, her eyes bulging and bright. 'I mean, she had on these amazing shoes! If I'd been closer to her I'd totally have asked her where she got them.'

Tilly felt like her friend was speaking another language. If she'd been fortunate to meet Cinderella she'd ask her what it was like to kiss a prince and attend a royal ball. Yet all Josephine had been concerned about were a pair of shoes.

'Was she wearing the glass slippers?' Tilly asked suddenly, realisation dawning on her. Of course Josephine would have wanted to ask about those, they were the most amazing pair of shoes either of them had ever seen. Both girls had professed as much.

'Of course not, silly.' Josephine laughed but it was warm and gentle, not mocking. 'She was in Jimmy Choos.'

'In what?'

'Oh my goodness, Tilly, I've missed you so much! I'd forgotten what a character you are!'

'I've missed you too. I was thinking –'

Josephine's head suddenly turned away from the screen. Tilly could make out muffled words in the background.

'I'm so sorry, but I've got to go,' Josephine told her as she snapped back towards her camera. For someone who was sorry she was smiling profusely.

'Poppy's called about tomorrow so I really need to talk to her. Bye, speak soon! Kisses!'

Josephine blew a kiss and then the screen was once again a sea of blue.

Leaning back in her chair, Tilly gazed at the screen. Now there was only the hum of the computer filling the room.

'So?' her mother spoke from the other end of the table. 'Was it nice speaking with Josephine?'

Tilly nodded slowly. 'Yeah. It was nice.'

She kept looking at the screen. Josephine had changed since the last time she'd seen her, and it wasn't just her hair. But Tilly was the same, still a 'character'. What if everyone around her continued to change and she was fated to remain the same – frozen in time like some forgotten princess?

You SHALL Go to the ball!

'A party?' Tilly turned around in surprise to face her mother, who had been plaiting her hair. Ivy firmly gripped her daughter's shoulders and spun her back around so they were both facing the mirror.

'Tilly, stay still until I'm finished.' Ivy's words were mumbled as she clenched had a hair band between her teeth.

'When is it?' Tilly was staring at her mother's reflection. She watched Ivy complete the plait and secure it with the band.

'Next Saturday.'

'Really? Wow.' Tilly climbed up onto the double bed to sit beside her mother. They were in her parent's bedroom, which always smelt of strong perfume.

'It was your dad's idea.' Ivy was nervously wringing her hands together.

'I think an anniversary party sounds really fun.' Tilly leaned against her mother. It was Sunday evening and she was willing the weekend not to end. 'How long have you and Dad been married?'

'Seventeen years,' her mother said softly.

'Seventeen years!' Tilly exclaimed. 'That's like ... forever.'

'Well, it's definitely something worth celebrating.'

'Who's coming?' Tilly could feel bubbles of excitement gathering inside her. Their last family party had been over two years ago when her older cousin, Gregg, turned eighteen.

'All the usual suspects,' her mother told her with a tight smile.

'Like Auntie Caron?'

'Yep.'

'And Uncle Stew?'

'Yes.'

'And Gregg and Alicia?'

'Yes, Tilly, everyone should be there.' Her mother was getting up and heading towards the bedroom door. Tilly wanted to stop her because once she walked out onto the landing she'd turn around and tell her daughter that it was time she went to bed. And once Tilly went to bed she was one step closer to Monday. Just thinking about a new school week made Tilly shudder.

'Will there be cake?' Tilly's voice was urgent even though her question wasn't. Ivy paused by the door.

'I think your gran is making a cake.'

Her mother pressed down on the handle.

'Sponge cake?'

'Probably fruit, I'm afraid.'

'Oh.' Tilly's shoulders sank. Unlike the adults in her family she failed to see the appeal of fruit cake. It was dense and not nearly as sweet as sponge cake.

'It's getting late.' Ivy was on the landing now, looking at the small wooden clock hanging on the far wall. 'You should get to bed.'

Tilly remained on her mother's bed, idly kicking her legs. The party was a new source of discussion, one she intended to exhaust before having to go to bed.

'Will there be music?'

'Your dad's friend, Steve, will probably DJ.'

'Will there be a buffet?'

'Tilly, come on. It's bed time.'

With a reluctant shove, Tilly launched herself off the bed and skulked over to her mother.

'Mum?' She titled her head to look up at her mother as she passed her.

'What, Tilly?' Ivy sighed.

'Seventeen years isn't an anniversary people normally have a party for, is it?'

Her mother pursed her lips and shook her head. 'It's not.'

'So how come you and Dad are?'

Something Tilly couldn't decipher flickered in her mother's eyes.

'You'll understand when you're older,' Ivy replied. 'Now go to bed.'

'Why wouldn't I understand now?' Tilly demanded, instantly wounded.

'Tilly, bed.' Her mother was pointing to the bedroom door on the other side of the landing.

'Fine.' Tilly lowered her head and took slow, pained footsteps over towards her bedroom.

'Why is the party on a Saturday night?' Monica asked at breakfast the next morning, clearly appalled by the news.

'Yeah, couldn't it be like a Friday or something?' Maria added.

Tilly had no answers. Her father was already at work whilst her mother was upstairs sleeping, leaving her to round up breakfast on her own. She was certain her parents had incorrectly assumed her sisters would intervene and help her out. Instead, all they were interested in was moaning.

'Mum said it was this Saturday,' Tilly explained as she carefully poured cereal into a bowl.

'I thought I heard her talking about it on the phone yesterday.' Monica thoughtfully pursed her lips.

'Aren't you excited?' Tilly asked, her eyes wide. She loved family parties. It was a chance for her older relatives to coo over her and tell her how much she'd grown. There was always cake, jelly, and too many sandwiches. People would talk and reminisce late into the night while Tilly got to spin around on the dance floor to her favourite songs.

'Excited?' Monica almost choked. 'Are you kidding? Family parties are the worst, they are unbelievably lame.'

'Maybe we don't have to go,' Maria said hopefully.

'Of course you have to go!' Tilly told them indignantly. 'It's for their seventeenth anniversary! They'll want you there.'

Her sisters shared a look but said nothing.

'Right, well, we'd better head off.' Monica smoothed on one final layer of lip gloss with her finger.

'Wait.' Tilly still hadn't finished eating her breakfast.

'For what?' Maria asked, one hand resting on her hip, the other clutching the strap of her school bag.

'For ... for me,' Tilly said. Monica's shiny lips twitched like was about to laugh.

'We're not walking with you,' Maria informed her. 'You need to find friends from your own year to walk with.'

Tilly glanced down helplessly at her bowl of cereal. She'd yet to succeed in making friends in her own year. She sat by Kate and her cronies in registration but she knew they hardly counted as friends, and moreover they'd never even consider walking to school with her.

'Hang on.' Monica was reaching into her bag. Items jangled from within as she rummaged around and she parted the top of the bag to peer inside.

'Come on,' Maria whined, jerking her head towards the door. 'We need to get going.'

'You can borrow this,' Monica pulled out an outdated iPod and threw it to Tilly. It landed on the table and skittered towards her.

'Where did you get that?' Maria demanded.

'Josh Rubens lent it to me.' Monica shrugged as her cheeks began to turn crimson.

Maria arched an eyebrow and stared at her sister. 'Why?' she demanded.

'Look, can we just get going?' Monica pleaded. Then she looked over at Tilly, who was tentatively reaching for the iPod.

'Listen to that when you're walking in. That way you won't feel so ... you know. Just make sure no one pinches it at school.'

'Yeah, cause who knows what you'd need to do for Josh Rubens then,' Maria teased.

'Shut up.' Monica gave her sister a sharp pinch on the upper arm. 'Make sure you leave in the next ten minutes else you'll be late,' she added with a backward glance. Tilly nodded, then her sisters were gone and she was alone with her breakfast.

Almost fifteen minutes later, Tilly was hurriedly locking up the front door. She'd loitered too long at the bottom of the stairs, considering shouting up to her mother to say goodbye but ultimately feared she'd wake her. And now she risked being late.

Her backpack swung on her shoulders as Tilly scurried down the driveway and began following the route her father normally drove to the school. It was only at the park that the synchronicity would end. Instead of going around it, as the cars had to, Tilly would be able to walk straight across.

As she walked she fumbled with the iPod Monica had given her. It took her several attempts to get it working. She inserted the ear buds and rock music instantly blasted into her brain. It was so loud it made the hair on the back of Tilly's neck stand up. She jumped, certain she'd almost gone deaf. The song continued though Tilly made sure to lower the volume. It was no wonder

Monica never heard anyone knocking on her bedroom door if she was listening to music this loudly.

Tilly recognised the song. It was one her sisters liked to play over and over again about a guy who had caught his girlfriend cheating. He seemed to enjoy singing about how awful she was and how he'd never take her back. Although it wasn't the sort of song Tilly would usually listen to, Monica was right in that it did make her feel significantly less alone. In her peripheral vision, she spied the tell-tale green of school jumpers but with music for company she wasn't as self-conscious as she'd usually be.

Once in the park, Tilly picked up the pace, aware she already risked being late. She hurried past the rusted swings that creaked even when there was no one on them. She had broken into a light run by the time she reached the broken down carousel. If it wasn't for the students loitering near it smoking, she might have stopped to reminisce. Instead, she scurried by with her personal soundtrack blasting in her ears.

With just one minute to spare Tilly arrived, the playground already growing empty as students filtered into the oppressive building. Gasping, Tilly quickly removed the iPod and shoved it into the base of her bag.

'What happened to you?' Kate asked with a smirk as Tilly sat down beside her. It was rare for the others to be seated before her.

'What?' Tilly asked as she slid off her backpack and placed it beneath her desk.

Kate scoffed, 'You look like you've been dragged through a hedge backwards.'

Blushing, Tilly lifted her hands to smooth down her hair. Long strands had broken free from her plait and blown madly about when she'd rushed through the park.

'Jeez, ever heard of hair spray?' Kate asked with malice as her friends snickered.

Cheeks burning, Tilly did her best to ignore them, silently vowing to check out the state of her hair when she went to the toilets.

'Did you hear Sons of Cherry are going on tour?' Sophie asked. Normally, Tilly would zone out the conversation but she recognised the name of the band. It was the song that had been on the iPod that morning.

'Of course I heard,' Kate said sharply. 'Everyone on earth has. Except maybe ...' Tilly could feel piercing blue eyes on her.

'Matilda,' Kate called. 'Do you know who Sons of Cherry are?'

Tilly wanted to carry on ignoring them – it had worked OK for her so far. But a part of her kept thinking about her Skype call with Josephine and what Maria had said. Maybe Tilly needed to start being more like everyone else if she wanted to be accepted.

'I know who they are,' Tilly said softly. 'They sing "Jezebel Walking".'

'Ooh, get you!' Claire cooed from the end of the desk. Tilly waited for Kate to say something, but instead she tightened her thin lips into a line and turned back towards her friends.

'So which of you is going to get me a ticket?'

'I can get one,' Sophie blurted a little too eagerly. 'Mum will let me use her credit card.'

'Sounds perfect,' Kate purred.

'Morning, class.' The door was pushed open and Miss Havishorn walked in, wearing the same brown cardigan she'd worn every day the previous week.

'How are we all?' No one replied as she

shuffled her way towards the front of the classroom.

'Talkative as ever,' Miss Havishorn laughed to herself. 'Well, let's crack on with another week, shall we?'

By Wednesday, Tilly knew all the words to "Jezebel Walking". Monica had yet to ask for the iPod back so Tilly continued to listen to it when she walked to school. Sometimes she listened to it in the evening. She was starting to find something relaxing about the lead singer's hoarse, emotion-filled voice.

'Are you getting excited for Saturday?' Tilly asked her mother, who was sat beside her at the dining table knitting a purple scarf, presumably for Monica since that was her favourite colour.

'Huh?' Ivy blinked as her long knitting needles ceased moving.

'Saturday?' Tilly leaned on her chair to peer at her mother. 'Are you excited for the party?'

Tilly was making the most of her allocated one hour's use of the computer for the evening. She was trying to get as much of her homework done as possible before her sisters descended upon it and started looking up Sons of Cherry videos and stalking the band on Twitter.

'Oh, yes.' Ivy smiled and nodded, staring blankly at the wool she was holding as though she'd forgotten what she was doing.

'What are you going to wear?' Tilly pressed. To her, the best bit about parties were always the outfits.

'Mmm?'

'What are you going to wear to the party, Mum?'

'Oh, I don't know.' Ivy dropped the needles and wool and pushed back her chair as if they were contaminated.

'I was thinking, could I wear my new princess dress?' Tilly wondered. By new, she meant most recently acquired. The dress had been a Christmas gift, which made it almost ten months old and considerably not new.

'Mmm, sure.' Ivy's hand floated absently through the air.

'Are you sure?' Tilly had now stopped typing altogether. When there was a small family gathering for Easter earlier in the year, Tilly had asked about wearing her princess dress and had been given a definite no in response. Apparently it wasn't a suitable outfit for anyone over the age of ten. Tilly instead had to wear a green velvet dress which had once belonged to both Monica and Maria and didn't even fit properly. The sleeves were too long, which meant Tilly had spent all day shoving them up to a reasonable length.

'Yeah, wear what you want,' Ivy said, standing up and smoothing her hands down the front of her jeans. 'I'm going to go upstairs and lie down for a bit.'

'OK.' Tilly shifted in her chair to gaze at the computer again.

'Tell your dad for me, OK?'

'Sure.'

Tilly could hardly wait to head upstairs and try on her dress. She wanted to stop doing her homework there and then but she knew how disappointed her parents would be if her school work didn't improve. She was doing her best to make up for the detention she'd got at the start of term.

She was just finishing typing up a short essay about Henry VIII's wives for her history class when the kitchen door opened, bringing with it the pleasant scent of freshly cooked chips.

'Tilly, can you set the table?' her father called. Tilly instantly ceased typing and got up to oblige. She'd quickly learned that when her dad was on early shifts his mood was much more volatile. The last thing she wanted was to give him cause to get mad at her.

'Yep.' Tilly headed to the sideboard which was older than she was to grab the faded yellow placemats.

'Where's your mum?' Clive asked, still lingering in the doorway, his eyes roaming across the empty table.

'She went upstairs for a lie down.'

Her father's grip tightened against the door. For a panicked moment, Tilly feared he was going to be mad. She braced herself for a tidal wave of angry words to wash over her but instead he returned to the heat of the kitchen.

Tilly's mother didn't come down for dinner, which seemed to contribute to her father's darkening mood.

'I'm wearing my princess dress on Saturday,' Tilly proudly told her sisters. Perhaps it was the taste of the chips or the prospect of dressing up like an actual princess but Tilly was in a decidedly good mood.

'Huh?' Monica frowned, a chip between her fingertips.

'On Saturday, I'm wearing my new princess dress.'

'Oh God, Saturday.' Maria rolled her eyes and sighed. 'Don't remind us.'

'Yeah, thanks, squirt.' Monica dropped her chip back on to her plate. 'The last thing we wanted to think about was that suck-fest.'

'Watch your mouth!' Their father's stern words rained down over them like a hail of bullets. Both Monica and Maria flinched.

'Saturday's party is important to your mother!' he insisted, the veins on his neck beginning to throb with worrying intensity.

Tilly felt her mouth drop open but she was wise enough not to speak. Her mother had said that it had been Dad's decision to throw the party.

'I want all three of you on your best behaviour!' Clive continued, glancing between each of them.

Tilly could feel her face growing hot. She'd only ever been excited about the party, why was her Dad grouping her in with his anger towards her sisters? It didn't seem fair.

'Dad, we're sorry.' Monica lowered her head to her plate to look at the pile of chips resting beside a half-eaten piece of battered fish.

'You know what this party means to your mother.' He was pointing at Monica with his fork, brandishing it like a weapon.

'Yes. I know.'

'Dad, we'll behave. Promise.' Maria added, sounding unusually sincere.

'Good.' Clive leaned back in his chair, seemingly appeased. Tilly continued to eat and waited for the dust to settle before speaking again.

'Did you hear Sons of Cherry are going on tour?' she asked her sisters, hoping they'd nod approvingly and maybe suggest they all go together.

'Everyone heard,' Monica replied quietly, casting a wary glance in their father's direction.

'Are you going to go?' Tilly wondered.

'Yeah,' Monica gave a stiff laugh, 'we've got front row seats.'

'Really?' Tilly could only imagine how jealous Kate would be if she knew.

'Jeez, squirt.' Maria was rolling her eyes. Thankfully, their father was too preoccupied with staring into space to pay any attention.

'You seriously need to grow up,' Monica said sternly.

Tilly flinched and leaned back in her chair, wondering what she'd done wrong.

Spinning around in the centre of her room, Tilly savoured how the light sparkled off her dress. It was bright blue and looked as though it had been dipped in ice. Wearing it made Tilly feel magical. She excitedly skipped across the landing to her mother's room, keen to show off.

'Mum, Mum, look!' Tilly called out as she walked in, not pausing to knock. She slowed when she noticed that the curtains were drawn. Approaching the bed, she could make out the shadow of her mother curled up on her side.

'Mum?'

'Oh, Tilly.' Ivy stretched and, with some effort, sat up. 'Did I miss dinner?'

'Yeah.' Tilly was staring at her mother, trying to understand why she was in bed. She couldn't possibly be tired; she slept in every morning.

'Is that your dress?' Her mother reached for Tilly's hand and used it to spin her around. Tilly obliged, her worries quickly forgotten.

'Don't you love it, Mum?'

'Yes,' Ivy said tenderly. 'You look just like a princess.'

'See, I've even got the plait.' Tilly tugged eagerly at her own hair.

'So you do.' Her mother was smiling and it cheered Tilly to see that it extended all the way to her eyes. 'You have such beautiful hair, Tilly.'

'Do you think?' Tilly climbed up on to the bed so she was sat beside her mother. She fingered the end of her plait, gazing at her mousy, brown hair.

'Of course,' Ivy enthused.

'Josephine straightens her hair so it looks like Monica's and Maria's. Should I straighten mine too?'

'No.' Her mother drew her close for a cuddle. 'Your hair is beautiful just the way it is.'

'Thanks, Mum.' Tilly nuzzled close. Her mother smelt of soap and mint. 'Do you know what you're wearing yet?'

'I don't.' She felt her mother shrug. 'I'll probably throw something on.'

'I like your black dress with the bow.' Tilly remembered the first time she'd seen her mother in the dress. Her parents had been heading out to a New Year's Eve party and when her mother had swept into the lounge to say goodbye she'd looked every inch the movie star. Her body was more voluptuous, her hair thicker. She was still beautiful, but like a painting that had been left in the sun. The radiance was still there but it had been dulled by time.

'I like that dress too,' her mother said, giving her a squeeze.

'You always look so beautiful in it,' Tilly said dreamily.

'Thank you, sweetheart. How's school? Is it a bit better now?'

'A bit.' Tilly was actually being truthful.

'See, I told you it would be.'

'It still kind of sucks,' Tilly admitted.

'You shouldn't talk like that.' Her mother gave her a tighter squeeze. 'It makes you sound like your sisters.'

'Maybe I should sound more like them,' Tilly sighed. 'I mean, they are both really popular.'

'There's more to life than being popular.'

'Like what?'

Her mother laughed lightly and leaned back, opening up the space between them.

'Like being happy,' she raised a thin hand to tuck away a loose strand of Tilly's hair.

'Popular people are happy.'

'Do your sisters seem happy to you?' her mother asked with a cheeky smile. 'They seem moody all the time to me.'

Tilly laughed.

'You need to promise that you won't spend too much time worrying what others think of you.' Her mother was staring intently at her and Tilly nodded numbly. It sounded like an impossible request.

'I'm serious,' Ivy continued, placing Tilly's hands between her own. Despite being in bed, she was as cold as ice.

'You're a special person, Tilly. You see the good in the world. I'd hate for you to ever lose that.'

'I thought I needed to grow up.'

'I don't know,' her mother sighed. 'Sometimes I think it's so important for you to grow up, and other times I wish you could stay safe in your fantasies forever.'

'I should just be happy, right?'

'Yes,' her mother was smiling. 'You should just be happy.'

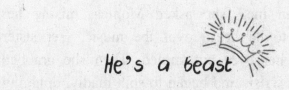

He's a beast

The disco lights made Tilly's dress sparkle as though she were the rarest of diamonds. The music booming from the DJ booth pounded in her ears as she spun around the dance floor. Even some of her aunts were up and gleefully shuffling around as the DJ played an old song from long before Tilly's was born.

It was after ten and the party was in full swing. The small room that backed onto their local pub was packed to capacity. Everyone was full of cake and high spirits. Tilly had been complimented on her princess dress five times. She'd been counting as she gathered together the kind words, clutching them tight to her chest.

Even Monica and Maria were dancing after some coaxing from their grandmother. Their outfits showed too much leg, which earned some raised eyebrows from older members of the Roberts brood.

Tilly was giggling happily as she went over to her sisters.

'Spin me,' she asked Monica, raising her voice to be heard over the music. Her sister rolled her eyes but smiled. Then she grabbed Tilly's wrists and began to spin madly, dragging her little sister along. It was a game they always used to play at family parties. Monica would spin Tilly until the lights started to blur and the room began to tilt.

As they parted, Tilly was laughing. She couldn't remember the last time she'd had so much fun with her sisters. Even her parents looked to be having a good time from where they were stood at the bar. For most of the evening they had been engaged in conversation with whoever had most recently walked through the door. But now her mother was throwing her head back and laughing heartily. She was wearing the black dress with the bow. It dipped too low at the back, revealing her shoulder blades protruding like vast mountain ranges.

Tilly stopped dancing and watched her mother

laugh. There was something magnetic about the way she was caught in the moment, her eyes crinkled and her hand resting casually on her husband's forearm. She was no longer just a mother; she was a beautiful woman at a party.

Tilly was still looking over as her father gestured towards the DJ booth. The music abruptly stopped and everyone glanced at one another uneasily.

'Sorry to interrupt.' Her father was walking towards the dance floor, leading his wife by the hand. 'Ivy and I wanted to say a few words.'

Monica's hands landed on Tilly's shoulders as she drew her sister to the edge of the space.

'First of all, thank you all for coming.' Clive was raising his voice so everyone in the room could hear him. Chatter had ceased as every pair of eyes honed in on him. 'Ivy and I are thrilled that so many of you could join us to celebrate our seventeenth anniversary.'

Someone sniffed loudly. Tilly grew up on to her tip toes to find the source of the sound. A few feet away she could see her grandmother sat at a table by the dance floor, a tissue pressed against her damp eyes.

'Yes, it really is so wonderful to see everyone,' Ivy gushed as she leaned against her husband.

'We love you, Ivy!' one of Tilly's uncles shouted drunkenly.

'I love you too.' Tilly's father was gazing adoringly into his wife's eyes, which fluttered prettily, framed by mascara-coated lashes. She was arguably wearing too much make up, but Tilly's sisters had insisted on helping their mother get ready.

'Thank you for the best seventeen years of my life.' Clive's voice was quiet, his words meant only for his wife. The couple kissed and the room erupted with thunderous applause. Tilly enthusiastically clapped her hands. She felt like she was standing in a real life fairy tale, watching the King and Queen as they enjoyed their happily ever after.

Instead of leather miniskirts, her sisters wore floor length silk gowns in shades of purple and blue. The small, dimly lit room, which had been hired for the event, extended into the banquet hall of a vast stone castle. Candelabras hung from the ceiling and huge bouquets of flowers were scattered about the room, filling the air with a heady floral fragrance. Gone was the DJ booth, in its place an elegant string quartet who, upon the King's order, commenced playing.

People came together, already knowing the steps to the dance. The soft tinkle of glasses placed upon trays and silver cutlery scraped against fine china provided a musical background. It was a perfect evening, one the residents of the Kingdom would talk about for years to come.

'Come on, squirt.' Maria was tugging her sister's hand, her face pinched and impatient.

'What?' Tilly shook her head. She was back in the dim room, which continued to smell like stale cigarettes even though people had to go outside to smoke.

'Aren't you gonna dance?' Maria was pulling Tilly towards the dance floor before she could protest. Strong, familiar chords were blaring out. The DJ was playing Sons of Cherry.

'Did you request this?' Tilly asked, eyes wide. She hadn't dared request any songs. She thought that as this was her parents' party the music should be songs that they liked. And they certainly weren't fans of Sons of Cherry.

'Of course!' Maria nodded, laughing. 'It's about time they played some real music!'

Monica was already enthusiastically moving in the centre of the dance floor. The numbers had dwindled as the older family members had scurried off to their tables at the first sound of something unfamiliar.

But Gregg was up and dancing, wrapping his arms around a girl with bright red hair who Tilly didn't recognise. She must have been his new girlfriend.

'Come on!' Maria urged, waving her arms about. Tilly tried to copy the movements though she doubted she looked as effortlessly cool as Maria did.

She was spinning around and shaking her hips when someone tapped her on the shoulder. She half expected it to be her father wearing one of his sternest expressions, telling her she should be dancing in a more ladylike fashion. But when Tilly turned around the red-haired girl was looking at her.

'Cute dress,' she exclaimed in an accent which sounded vaguely Irish.

'Thank you.' Tilly gave a quick pirouette on

the spot. As she spun the fabric fanned out and billowed around her legs.

'I love it!' The red-haired girl clasped a hand to her chest. 'You're, like, the cutest thing ever.'

'George, this is my cousin, Tilly.' Gregg stepped forward, one hand still draped around the redhead's slim waist. 'Tilly, this is Georgina.'

'Hi,' Tilly gushed. She couldn't believe that someone so much more sophisticated than she was would like her dress so much. If Georgina was with Gregg then she was older than Monica and Maria – probably at university like he was.

'You're so sweet.' Georgina reached out and placed a hand on Tilly's shoulder. Her nails were painted jet black as though she'd dipped her fingers in ink. 'I'm sorry about –'

Gregg sharply hoisted her away and whispered something into Georgina's ear. When she looked back, her expression had changed. She looked troubled.

'It's an awesome dress,' she smiled as Gregg edged her to another part of the dance floor.

Tilly watched them walk away, wondering what Gregg had whispered to his girlfriend. Had he said something mean about Tilly? That wasn't

143

like him. He'd always been so nice.

'Hey, come on. You're supposed to be dancing.' Tilly was pulled towards the centre of the dance floor. Her sisters wedged her between them as they danced around, swaying their arms.

'I can't believe we're meant to dance all night,' Maria said above Tilly's head.

'Yeah, my feet are already killing me,' Monica moaned. Tilly looked down and noticed the staggering height of her sister's shoes. She was wearing black stilettos covered in bright pink spikes. They looked funky but threatening, much like Monica often did.

'It was nice of Amy to lend you those shoes,' Maria continued.

'At first I thought it was,' Monica said between breaths, 'but now I think it might be a punishment for what happened between me and Jake last year.'

This made Maria laugh.

'Amy's always been jealous.'

'Too right. You know what, stuff it.' Monica dramatically kicked off her shoes, sending them skittering across the polished floor and towards the table where their grandmother was sitting. The silver-haired lady lowered her crinkled face to look at the shoes as though they were from another planet.

'That's better,' Monica sighed, now much closer to Tilly's height. 'I can't keep wearing those shoes.'

'Why does Dad want us to dance all night?' Tilly asked. Both sisters ceased moving and looked at her in surprise, as if they'd momentarily forgotten she was there.

'He just wants to make sure everyone is having a good time,' Monica coolly explained.

Maria was nodding. Her tense expression was framed by her sleek hair, which had been straightened with militant precision.

Monica's hair was fashioned in the same style. From behind, it would be impossible to tell the two sisters apart. Tilly didn't look like she had swum out of the same gene pool. She was much shorter. Her hair was plaited down her back and her fresh-faced look had been created with only soap and water.

Monica and Maria both wore dark eyeliner, bright lipstick, and heaps of foundation. Their nails were freshly painted in dark shades and they smelt as though they'd fallen into a vat of perfume. They wore matching tight skirts but

Monica was wearing a clingy Sons of Cherry T-shirt and Maria had on a modest black vest. As always, they were beautiful. Tilly doubted she'd ever look as amazing as them no matter how much makeup she wore or how tight her clothes were.

'Dad wants the party to be great.' Maria was lifting Tilly's arms and manoeuvring her about. An up-tempo song was playing but not all of the guests had flocked to the dance floor.

'We should request the Grease mega-mix or something to try and get everyone dancing,' Monica shouted to her sister, who rolled her eyes in disgust.

'I'll do it!' Tilly offered helpfully.

'Go for it, squirt.' Maria released her grip and Tilly skipped over to the DJ booth.

By the end of "Summer Nights" and its impossibly high note, almost everyone was on the dance floor. The space around Tilly quickly started to reek of alcohol but she didn't care, she was having too much fun. She was finally out on a Saturday night. When Monday rolled around she'd actually have something to say to Kate and her friends when they sarcastically asked about her weekend.

'Actually, I went to a party,' Tilly could imagine herself saying. 'And I danced all night and it was amazing.'

Her gathered aunts, uncles, and cousins were singing along, drunkenly embracing one another and swaying side to side. Even Tilly's parents had been gathered up in the mix. Everyone had come together, everyone was having fun. Tilly considered that if getting married meant you got to have anniversary parties like this then it was definitely worth doing.

Tilly felt unsettled in the stillness of her bedroom. She was back in her tower but she could feel the burn of the disco lights in her eyes, the roar of music in her ears. She wished she was on the dance floor, spinning around with her sisters. Her princess dress was now tucked away in a drawer. Her nightdress was softer but she missed the brilliant sparkle of the dress' fabric.

With a sigh, Tilly rolled onto her back and gazed at the stars on her ceiling. They glowed dimly, arranged in the constellations that shone over Tilly's kingdom. She felt happy that peace had been restored through the land. The grand ball at the castle had ensured the happiness of her townspeople but still Tilly couldn't sleep. Her heart beat anxiously in her chest, urging her to get up.

After staring at the stars for twenty minutes, Tilly pushed off her duvet cover with a groan and sat up, her head almost grazing the ceiling. Soon she would be too tall to sleep on the top bunk. Most of the darkness in her room was absorbed by the streetlight beyond her window which glowed through her curtains. She liked to think of it as her own personal night light.

Distantly, Tilly heard a muffled sound. It was so soft she almost missed it. But when it came again her senses sharpened with certainty. Tilly eased herself down from her tower quietly and landed softly on her carpeted floor. On her tip toes she crept to her door and placed her ear against it. The sound was slightly louder now. It sounded like someone struggling to catch their breath. As Tilly held her own she pushed on her door handle and moved into the landing. Her eyes had to adjust to the increased darkness but the glow beneath the bathroom door provided a guiding light.

Taking careful, deliberate steps, Tilly approached the bathroom door. The sound was much clearer. It wasn't someone struggling to breathe – it was someone sobbing. For a moment, Tilly was stunned, frozen with indecision. She'd never heard someone cry like this at home before. It was late. Everyone else was tucked up in bed, lost to their dreams. Only Tilly and the person in the bathroom were awake. Their pained sobbing troubled Tilly immensely. She didn't know if she could help them, she just knew she had to try.

Without knocking, Tilly opened the bathroom door. Bright light bled out into the space, causing her to squint and raise a hand against her eyes. As the sudden glare receded, Tilly saw her father stooped over the bathroom sink, both hands gripping its ceramic edges for support. His shoulders were shaking as he turned to look at her with raw eyes. His cheeks were slick with tears and he was still wearing his smart trousers, shirt, and tie from the party.

'Dad, are you OK?' Tilly took a tentative step forward.

'Tilly, get to bed.' He barked the words as he turned away.

'Dad, you're crying.' She was just a few inches away from him now. His clothes carried the scent of stale cigarettes and alcohol. Was he sick? Tilly remembered a few months ago when her father had gone out drinking with friends and come back late. She'd woken up to the sound of him vomiting but when she'd gone to investigate further, Mum was already up and guarding the bathroom door.

'Your father has a stomach bug,' she'd told Tilly, her face as white as a sheet. 'Go on back to bed, sweetheart.'

Only he didn't have a stomach bug. She'd heard her sisters talking the next morning about how hungover their father was.

'If we came in and pulled a stunt like that he'd kill us,' Monica declared, her words dripping with venom.

'It's always the same,' Maria agreed fervently, 'one rule for him and another for the rest of us.'

But Tilly's father wasn't being sick now. He was crying. It was different.

'Didn't you enjoy the party?' Tilly wondered meekly.

'Fuck.' Clive gasped out the word and remained facing the wall. Tilly tensed on hearing the expletive. Such a word was forbidden inside the house. If her father had heard one of his children use it he'd have cut out their tongue.

'Dad, what's wrong?'

'Everything!' her father roared, finally looking at her. His eyes were wide and unfamiliar. 'Everything's wrong, Matilda! How can you not get that? This whole world is completely fucked up!'

Tilly was staggering backwards. What had she done to make him so mad at her?

'You're … you're in this ridiculous cocoon of imaginary stories while the rest of us are struggling to just … cope!'

Tilly stared fearfully at her father's contorted face, his lips curled up with contempt. Who was this man? It wasn't her dad. This man was some sort of beast.

'Daddy.' Tilly coughed as hot tears began to burn their way down her cheeks. She shook underneath the flimsy fabric of her nightdress. She'd only come to check he was OK. Why was he this angry?

'Daddy.' Clive grimaced as he echoed the

word. 'Daddy!' His voice was so loud now that his words crashed against Tilly with the force of a brick wall. 'You need to grow up, Matilda! You're twelve years old, for God's sake! Maybe if you weren't such a baby things would be easier around here!'

So he was crying because of her? Tilly couldn't stop shaking. It made no sense. Her dad loved her, didn't he? She glanced fearfully in the direction of her parent's bedroom door, where her mother was sleeping. Why wasn't she waking up? Why wasn't she hurrying to Tilly's defence?

'Don't even think about waking her up!' Clive raged. 'She already uses up enough energy looking out for you!'

Tilly was sobbing, her chest involuntarily heaving. If only she'd just stayed in her bedroom she wouldn't have had to hear these ugly words.

'Just go to bed!' Clive boomed before turning away again. Tilly didn't wait for him to tell her twice. Her little legs carried her across the landing, back to the safety of her bedroom as fast as they could. With her chest still heaving, Tilly slammed her door shut and breathlessly leaned against it. She raised a hand and wiped away some of her tears.

She was being chased by a fire-breathing dragon. She had to escape, and fast. Gathering up her long skirt, Tilly ran towards her stone tower. The structure stretched up high towards the shimmering stars. Tilly reached forward to get a foothold and stopped. She could distantly hear the dragon snarling. What if it came after her and cornered her atop her tower? All it would take was one fiery breath to destroy Tilly.

No, the tower was no longer safe. Pausing, she tried to think fast. She was out in the open and vulnerable but where could she go? Every second she wasted allowed the dragon to gain on her. And she refused to be dinner for the beast.

'Think, think,' Tilly urged herself as she stood in the darkness, her hands tightly clenched at her side.

She remembered hearing of a place where all lost children were welcome; a place where adults didn't rule, a place where you could be free. Fuelled with determination, Tilly sprinted to her window and threw open the curtains. The stars in the night sky were almost drowned out completely by the burning orb of the street lamp. But they were still there, like faint dots on a map.

She knew where she had to go, what she had to do. Stretching up, she opened her window. Cool air breezed in and tickled Tilly's bare legs. She searched for one particularly star, but thanks to the street lamp it was obscured from view. But it didn't matter. Tilly would find it soon enough.

Out on the landing a door slammed so loudly that it sounded like a gun shot. Tilly tensed and moved towards her bunk bed, lowering herself into the tight space between it and the carpet. Disturbed dust exploded in her face as Tilly wiggled her way towards the wall. Her hands moved over loose change and lost toys but in the darkness, Tilly couldn't examine what she was feeling.

Pressed tightly against the ground, Tilly waited, expecting a beam of light to fall across the floor as her bedroom door was opened. She wasn't really sure why she felt compelled to hide. She just knew that her father had to be avoided. His words had been seared into her mind and made each breath feel pained. Did he truly resent Tilly for not growing up quickly enough?

She was crying again, her tears soaking into the dusty carpet. She waited for what felt like an eternity but her door didn't open. She heard another distant slam, less forceful this time. Her father must have gone to bed. He hadn't bothered to apologise for his harsh words.

Slowly, Tilly scrambled out from under her bed and knocked off the dust that had collected on her nightdress. With only the light from the street lamp to guide her, she went to her chest of drawers and retrieved the princess dress she'd only put away a few hours earlier. She managed to smile despite the sorrow in her heart.

'I'm sorry I couldn't grow up,' Tilly whispered to the unfeeling night. She stepped out of her nightdress and pulled on her princess dress as well as some thick tights and fresh pants. Then, still shivering from the sharp air filtering in through her open window, she rummaged around for her fur-hooded coat and pink Wellington boots.

Tilly grabbed her pink school backpack and began filling it with essential items; two stuffed toys, one of her pillows, and several DVDs. Her father had made it perfectly clear that she didn't belong at home anymore.

As she scrambled towards her window, Tilly sent a regretful look to her bedroom door. If only she could say goodbye to her mother. But she slept with the dragon by her side and Tilly couldn't risk awakening the beast.

Tilly positioned herself so that she was sat on her window ledge, her legs kicking against the outer wall. The street was eerily quiet, nearby houses in complete darkness. It felt like the entire world was sleeping except for Tilly. From her window it was just a short drop to the flat extended roof of the kitchen below.

A cool breeze pressed against Tilly, almost urging her to go back inside but she ignored it. She checked that her backpack was securely in place and, taking a deep breath, she dropped down.

Second Star to the Right and Straight on until Morning

Tilly landed against the roof with a dense thud. Luckily, no one was in the kitchen below else they'd have surely heard her. With as much stealth as she could muster, she scrambled to her feet and carefully plotted her way to the edge of the roof. Moss covered most of the roof like a deep green carpet. Tilly reached the end and peered at the cracked tarmac of the small driveway. She was still at least six feet from the ground without anything soft she could land on.

Looking back up at her open window, she could faintly make out the lines of her curtains trembling in the breeze.

'Come on,' Tilly urged herself, her words fogging in a light mist. She lowered herself against the roof, facing the house. Reaching for the drain pipe she secured her hands amongst the damp leaves gathered within it. Tilly tensed as she felt something scurry across her fingers but she managed not to scream. She was wedged at the end of the roof like a swimmer poised before a race at the edge of the pool. But she wasn't about to push off with her legs – instead, she released them so she was hanging by her fingertips. Her booted feet knocked against the glass of the kitchen window. Now all she had to do was let go.

Tilly closed her eyes and imagined that she was dropping onto a cloud. Her fingers released the drain pipe and a second later, her face connected with the rough driveway. Tilly gasped as the fall knocked the air out of her lungs. The ground felt hard and indifferent beneath her. As she shakily climbed to her feet, Tilly felt a deep ache in her leg and the flame of a fresh cut on her cheek. When she examined her face her fingertips came away stained with blood.

More than anything Tilly wanted to run to the glass-fronted door and hammer on it until someone let her in. She could go back to the warmth of her bed, have her wounds bathed and plastered. But what would her father think? If he found her crying on the doorstep like a baby it'd only further fuel his anger. No, Tilly couldn't go back.

Sucking in her tears, Tilly adjusted her backpack and began to walk down the driveway.

The street her family lived on was eerily still. Houses were shrouded in darkness, their curtains drawn tightly closed. Cars were idle in driveways and only the wind whispered as it blew past Tilly, tangling itself up in her already dishevelled hair.

Lowering her head against the wind, Tilly walked. Forcing one foot in front of the other she moved without daring to look back.

A cat almost as black as night darted out in front of her, pausing briefly to stare, its wide eyes reflecting the yellow from the street light. Tilly knew the cat. He was called Thomas and he lived two doors down with Mrs Bradshaw. Thomas' yowls regularly interrupted the stillness of the night as he fiercely fought to defend his territory.

'That damn cat has been in our garden again,' Tilly's father would sigh. 'He always comes round here, leaving mess everywhere.'

'Leave him be, Clive,' Tilly's mother would urge.

'You're not the one trying to weed, and digging up what he's already buried!' Tilly's father raged.

'Mum, can we get a cat?' Tilly asked. She liked how on hot days Thomas would stretch out on their small lawn, exposing his belly to the rays of the sun. And when Tilly tickled his belly he purred so loudly he sounded like her father's lawnmower.

'No.'

'Yes.'

Both her parents had answered at the same time.

'No,' her father was the first to repeat. 'Cats make too much mess.'

'I'd like a cat,' Tilly's mother said with a smile.

'How do you think he'd take to them?' Clive nodded at the garden. 'This whole street is Thomas' territory. You think he'd welcome a new cat? You've heard the way he fights. The little sod has even hissed at me once or twice.'

Thomas had never hissed at Tilly. She liked to think they shared some sort of secret bond, that

Thomas was only nice towards her because he knew she was actually a princess and he was an enchanted cat who would one day return to his human form.

Thomas mewed at Tilly. The sound was plaintive yet affectionate.

'Hey, Thomas.' Tilly bent down and reached for his soft fur. She stroked his chin as he enthusiastically leaned against her.

'You're such a good boy,' Tilly told him affectionately. 'I bet you're wondering what I'm doing out so late.'

Thomas didn't seem troubled by her presence. He seemed more interested in the fuss he was receiving.

'OK, OK, I've got to go now.' Tilly straightened and Thomas gazed up at her before releasing a single pleading mew.

'I can't stay,' Tilly explained with a shake of her head. 'My dad is too angry at me.'

Tilly continued walking down the street. She was almost at the point where the road forked and she'd be forced to choose which way to go. Thomas stalked her every step, trotting beside her in the shadows. It comforted Tilly to know he was there.

At the end of the road, Tilly paused and glanced in both directions. She had no idea where she was going. Like a lost soul at sea she'd been hoping that the stars would guide her but they remained obscured by the glare of the street lights.

'Which way?' Tilly wondered aloud. If she went left she would be pulled deeper into a housing estate filled with countless homes like her own. It was a warren of driveways and dead ends. If she went right she would pass by the park and beyond that, her school.

Tilly began moving before her mind had registered that she'd made a decision. She went right. Thomas loitered at the fork in the road, his head tilted in her direction inquisitively. Pausing, Tilly glanced back at him.

'Are you coming?' she asked.

Thomas remained regally sat on his back legs, his tail curled around him.

'Suit yourself.' Tilly turned away and continued trudging down the road. She saw the distant glow of headlights like bright eyes in the darkness. For a moment, she panicked. What if the driver pulled up and asked why she was out so late? What excuse could she give?

'I'm out for an evening stroll,' she could tell them sarcastically. As if they'd believe that. They'd probably report her to the police, which would result in a shameful homecoming. Her father would well and truly hate her then, and she could only imagine how mortified her mother would be if a patrol car pulled up outside and hauled Tilly out of the back.

But what if the driver wasn't that concerned about her safety? What if they were the sort of person who lingered too close to playgrounds and harboured dark intentions? It was only a few years ago that Dullerton's residents had been shaken when a little girl was abducted. She was only five. After ten days she was found in the woods on the outskirts of town.

Tilly only vaguely remembered the story. Her parents had watched the news with pale faces each night and demanded that none of the girls linger on their way home from school. Olivia White was the little girl's name. People lit candles in their windows and at school in assembly the students were encouraged to pray for her. But when they found her it was too late.

The wind grew sharper and Tilly shivered, tightening her coat around her.

'They never found them, you know,' Monica had told Tilly last Halloween.

'Found who?' Tilly asked, her frown barely visible underneath a layer of face paint. Tilly was going out dressed as a ghost, which meant that her face was painted white and she would be hidden beneath an old sheet with two eye holes cut out.

Monica smiled, and dropped a hand to her waist. She suited the cat outfit she was wearing. A dark mask covered her eyes and whiskers drawn on with eyeliner were strewn across her cheeks. A long fabric tail jutted out from a pair of leather hot pants. Even though she was meant to be scary she still managed to look sexy.

'The man who killed that little girl.' Behind her mask, Monica's eyes became bright with mischief.

'You're lying,' Tilly pouted.

'I'm not.' Monica purred and playfully spun her tail in her hand. 'Why do you think Mum and Dad are so twitchy about you going out trick or treating with Josephine?'

It was true that her parents were nervous, but they always had been. They didn't live in the securest of neighbourhoods.

'Monica, stop fibbing, you're just trying to scare me.' Tilly defiantly folded her arms across her chest.

'Fine, suit yourself.' Her sister shrugged as she began slinking her way out of the kitchen. She paused at the door, her purple lips drawn into a wicked smile.

'Apparently you can still hear her screams coming out of the woods.'

'Stop it!'

Monica was laughing as she left. Tilly was trembling. She didn't go out trick or treating that night – she talked Josephine into staying in and watching Hocus Pocus instead.

Tilly's heart was almost in her throat when the headlights ahead swiftly changed direction and the car pulled down a street. She felt her muscles become slack with relief.

'That was close,' she muttered to herself. She cast a fearful look down the road, hoping Thomas was still there. But he was gone, the path behind her completely bare.

Tilly knew she had to get away from the roads. That car hadn't gone past but she might not be so lucky with the next one. If she kept walking she'd soon reach the park. The darkness in there would be almost impenetrable away from street lights but Tilly would be safe from prying eyes.

She thought of the little girl who had gone missing and fear sliced up her spine like an ice pick.

'You can do this,' Tilly told herself sternly. 'Just grow up.'

Because that was what growing up was about, wasn't it? Facing your fears? Tilly moved as if on auto-pilot. Her limbs knew the way towards the park, towards the broken down carousel which lay at its centre. It was a route Tilly had walked countless times.

She remembered it most fondly when she skipped along in the sunshine, a hand securely held in her mother's grip. As soon as they reached the edge of the park she could hear the distant chimes of the carousel, and butterflies would dart around in her belly.

'Mummy, Mummy, can I ride? Please!' Tilly would jump up and down with excitement.

'Of course, sweetheart,' Ivy would reply, her words bathed in warmth. She'd reach in her purse and slip a shiny twenty pence piece into Tilly's tiny outstretched palm. That was all it cost to ride the carousel then, a mere twenty pence. But at six years old, twenty pence felt like a million pounds. Clutching the coin like a rare jewel, Tilly left her mother's side and eagerly ran deep into the park.

A line of children snaked away from a nearby ice cream van. People giggled as they kicked their legs on the swings or bounced on the see-saw. But Tilly only had eyes for the carousel. The sun gleamed off its golden surface as the ornate horses and carriages slowly spun around, accompanied by magical music.

'Will you ride?' a man with leathery skin in a red pinstripe shirt asked. Tilly nodded as she handed him her coin.

'Yes, please, Burt.'

'Right this way.' Burt unlocked a small golden gate and allowed Tilly to join the eager queue of children waiting for their turn.

'Afternoon Mrs Johnson,' Tilly heard Burt greet her mother, who arrived a few moments later.

'Afternoon, Burt. Has it been busy?'

'So-so.'

Tilly's mother continued chatting to Burt. Apparently he used to work with her father. But for Tilly, their conversation was drowned out by the mesmerising dance of the carousel horses. They were frozen in a gallop, their rainbow-coloured manes pushed back against an invisible wind.

Tilly always favoured the pink horses although, as they were one of the most popular, the brilliant shade of their reigns had been worn away in places.

The music stopped and the carousel stilled. Tilly began to lift her weight from foot to foot in an attempt to manage her growing impatience.

'Oh, excuse me.' Behind her, Burt excused himself from her mother so he could let on the new riders. Tilly hurried on after the others, her movements as direct as a missile. She was aiming for the pink horse at the back, the one reared up that looked like it was smiling.

Her hands hungrily grabbed it, claiming it as hers for the next three minutes. Then came the difficult task of climbing up. Tilly was shorter than other children her age. She could easily have been mistaken for four. Luckily, Burt was swiftly on hand to help.

'Up you get.' His hands reached underneath her armpits as she floor disappeared beneath her feet. Then she was atop her beloved horse, stretching her legs to full extent so she was able to place her feet in the stirrups.

'There you go.' Burt gave her a friendly wink as he moved on to aid someone else.

'I'm back,' Tilly whispered to her horse as she stroked its ceramic mane. Leaning forward, she held onto the golden spine which bound the animal to the carousel. And then the music started and the park began to spin. Tilly was now out on the open plains of her beloved Kingdom, riding her favourite horse. Together, they powered across the lands, not caring as the wind pushed their hair and pinked Tilly's cheeks. They were free and the world was their own.

Yet all too soon the spell was broken. The carousel slowed and Tilly gave a reluctant wave to her mother, praying she had another twenty pence piece in her purse.

After wandering in the darkness for ten minutes, Tilly arrived at the carousel. Time had performed a devastating dance with the ride. The mirrors at the centre were cracked, casting hideous reflections of the broken horses gathered around it. Only one or two horses remained erect on their spires. The others had come crashing down and were missing legs or had enormous holes which revealed their dark, hollow interior. Weeds had sprouted all over the carousel floor and hungrily weaved their way around the horses and into the three carriages. The ornate roof was broken in several places, letting moonlight filter on the sad scene.

Tilly blinked as she looked at the carousel, wishing there was some way she could wave a magic wand and restore it to its former glory. Now more than ever she needed to hear its soothing music and allow it to transport her to another world.

'No one goes on it anymore,' Maria had once scoffed when Tilly asked why the carousel was abandoned.

'Why?'

'Because the creepy old man who ran it disappeared.'

'Burt isn't creepy.' Tilly declared angrily. Burt was kind and a friend of their late grandfather.

'He still disappeared,' Maria shrugged.

'Where did he go?'

'Jeez, squirt.' Maria rolled her eyes. 'If people knew that they wouldn't say he disappeared!'

Unlike Olivia White, no one really cared when Burt disappeared. They ignored the carousel so it became dilapidated and a shadow of its former self.

'One day you'll sparkle again,' Tilly promised the ride. In the darkness it didn't look inviting. It looked downright foreboding. Dense shadows dwelled where there once had been golden spires and colourful horses.

Tilly inhaled sharply and stepped onto the carousel. The floor creaked angrily in protest as somewhere deep inside the ride she heard metal screech. It was obviously unsafe but she'd seen students draped inside it smoking so she was confident it would hold her weight.

It was hard to pick her footsteps without a light. There was debris all over the base of the carousel. Twigs, splintered glass, and cigarette ends all crunched beneath Tilly's boots as she carefully navigated her way to the far side. She knew where she was headed: to the carriage beside her favourite horse. The carriage she used to dream she'd one day ride in when she got married.

Tilly used to fantasise about the day she found her prince. Together they would ride the carousel and it would be adorned with wild flowers as the tinny music, that always played when it spun, twanged out the wedding march. But as Tilly shoved aside a fallen part of a broken horse she realised her dream would never come true. The carousel from her memory was gone and in its place stood a carcass which nature was hungrily feeding upon.

Her hand reached out and found the carriage. It had once been white with gold trimmings. Delicate pink flowers curled up the sides and inside there was one long seat carved to look like it was made of something soft. Taking off her backpack, Tilly tossed it into the carriage. The structure shook precariously as it landed but made no other sound. Tilly half expected to find a family of rats residing inside but it appeared to be empty. Gripping the sides of the carriage Tilly clamoured inside. In the darkness it was difficult to tell how it had fared over the years compared to the rest of the carousel. But Tilly was there and that was all that mattered. It was where she belonged.

Squashing up her backpack to the far side, she

leaned against it and gazed at the stars were exposed through a break in the roof. The moonlight that filtered in showed Tilly some of the images that had managed to survive around her. She could make out some of the cherubs painted on the underside of the roof, the decorated panel beside a cracked mirror which showed a beautiful castle atop a hill of green.

She shivered as the cool of the night began to seep through her clothes. Even though she was dressed warmly her skin was starting to prickle. At least it wasn't raining. Tilly doubted the carousel would provide ample shelter in a storm. She pressed herself against her backpack, using it as a makeshift pillow. She had no idea what the following day would bring, where she would go. She just knew she had been drawn to her beloved carousel. Perhaps she had hoped, that by some miracle, it would work again and spirit her away to a distant, magical world. But as the metal around her contracted and creaked it was a painful reminder that there would be no miracle. No happy ending. Tilly's carousel was very much broken and that was how it would remain.

Tilly awoke with a start, her heart pounding like a jack hammer. For a few precious seconds she thought she was back home, safe and warm in her bed. But as the cold pressed against her she remembered where she was. Glancing around at her bleak surroundings, Tilly tried to figure out what had woken her so suddenly. As her eyes scanned the shadows she became certain that she was very much alone.

A scream. Tilly winced as the sound echoed in her mind. She'd heard someone screaming. But had Tilly heard it or dreamt it?

'On a clear night you can still hear her screams coming out of the woods.'

Monica's declaration bubbled up from Tilly's memories.

'No.' Tilly shook her head and clamped her hands over her ears. 'I dreamt it. It's not real.'

Tilly drew her legs up to her chest, making herself into a tight, impenetrable ball. She'd thought she'd feel safe in her carriage but she was afraid. Fear held her heart in an icy vice, making each breath pained.

'Why did I come here?' Tilly asked herself,

squeezing her eyes shut. She could be sleeping soundly in bed instead of scared and alone in a broken down carousel. Hot tears wormed their way down her frozen cheeks.

'I don't want to grow up,' Tilly admitted as her shoulders began to shake, both from sorrow and the cold. Growing up meant she had to accept that magic couldn't endure. In her memories, the carousel glittered as though Midas himself had touched it. But now it was a death trap, something the people of Dullerton would rather tear down than restore. Why would Burt ever leave it? It was his pride and joy.

The shrill cry of a fox echoed through the park and Tilly held her breath. It sounded like a baby crying. It was brutal and terrifying and made her not dare to open her eyes. She knew it was a fox, she'd heard them before. But what if it was actually the ghost of Olivia White? What if she really could be heard on clear nights?

Tilly buried her head in her heads and tucked herself against her backpack. She was a veritable lost child with nowhere to go and no star to guide her home. This wasn't what was supposed to happen – in the pages of fairy tales she'd be rescued by a boy who wouldn't grow up or fairies who would take her in and make her one of their own. No one came.

Tilly eventually fell asleep and the shadows gathered in the carousel receded as dawn crept over the horizon, bleeding out across the sky.

Seaweed is Always Greener

Sunlight burned Tilly's eyes. Stretching, she wearily rubbed them. As the fog of sleep began to dissolve she realised how much her body ached. Her bones throbbed and her muscles burned. She felt like a spring that had been left too long in its box and desperately needed to extend. Straightening, Tilly sat up and stretched her arms high above her head, which alleviated some of her discomfort. But no matter how much she massaged her neck there was no removing the stiffness from it.

Glancing around, she saw more of the carousel in the tentative new light of day. Dark circles of rust chewed away at the still-standing horses, small pools of rain water gathered in crevices on the floor. Luckily, the sky exposed in

177

the break in the roof looked to be clear and blue.

Rubbing her eyes and yawning, Tilly wondered what time it was. The chill in the air told her it was still early. Dew clung to some of the weeds scattered throughout the carousel. Were her family even up? Did they know that she was missing?

Tilly imagined the bedlam that would ensue in the household when it was discovered that she was gone. There would be raised voices and tense questions. Would her father feel guilty?

Tilly sagged against the hard side of the carriage, suddenly weighed down with guilt. Her family would be beside themselves with worry. They'd call the police. Tilly strained to listen for the tell-tale screech of a siren patrolling the streets of Dullerton to find her. Glancing up, Tilly half expected to see a helicopter pass across the open patch of sky. But instead the morning was still and peaceful.

'Maybe they won't care,' Tilly mumbled as she stood up to stretch her legs. She didn't even know if she wanted to be found. If she went back, her parents would be mad. She already feared having to face her father again. Besides, he wouldn't want her to come home. One night spent sleeping beneath the stars hadn't made Tilly grow up. And that was what he wanted, wasn't it? –For her to grow up.

Tilly blinked back tears as she thought of what would be happening in her home on a typical Sunday morning. The house would smell like cooked bacon. Monica and Maria would sit with their fried sandwiches on their laps watching television, chatting about the night before. Tilly would prop herself up on a nearby chair, eagerly dipping soldiers into a runny egg. Everything always felt peaceful on Sunday mornings, with the whole family settling into a temporary sense of harmony.

By the afternoon the bacon scent would be replaced by the smell of roasted meat, either beef or chicken. Pans would be bubbling as they boiled vegetables and in the oven Yorkshire puddings would be rising. Tilly's stomach growled at the thought.

'Oww.' Tilly placed a hand to her tummy. She was starving.

Reaching round, she grabbed and unzipped her backpack. After a quick rummage, she found the packet of crisps she'd been searching for. It was hardly a bacon sandwich or boiled egg but it was all she had. As Tilly crunched on the salted crisps she wondered what the day held for her. Would she stay in the park or would she dare to venture further away from Dullerton? She wasn't even sure she knew the way out of town.

The carousel creaked wearily as the morning sunlight warmed its rusted frame. Tilly ran a hand along the side of the carriage. She wanted to stay in it forever. It felt safe despite its level of dilapidation. Beyond the carousel the world was vast and unfamiliar. Tilly didn't want to spend the rest of her life aimlessly wandering around but what choice did she have?

Still the morning was quiet and tranquil. Where were the helicopters? The sirens? Why was no one searching for Tilly? Her breath caught in her throat, causing her to almost choke on a crisp. What if they weren't looking for her? What if upon finding her empty bed and open window her family had just shrugged and accepted that she was gone? What if they didn't want her back?

Tilly pushed her empty crisp packet into her backpack and drew her knees up to her chest. She felt completely alone. She didn't even have a mobile so she could call Josephine. Even though her best friend had changed, she was still Tilly's best friend. Just to hear her voice would be a comfort. Instead, Tilly had the fractured carousel horses for company. Their empty black eyes gazed at her with indifference, their chipped ears and rusted sides a painful reminder of how easily something loved and cherished could be forgotten.

'They're not coming,' Tilly deduced to herself. She re-opened her backpack and pulled out a small stuffed unicorn which she clutched fiercely to her chest. As she nuzzled against it she realised it smelt of home. She hadn't even realised her home had a smell but it did. It smelt of vanilla, cooked meats, and polish. A lifetime of memories condensed in to one unmistakeable odour. Salty tears fell against her unicorn. Why was no one coming for her? Was she destined to forever be alone?

'There you are!'

Tilly jolted as she heard footsteps. The uneven floor was cracking angrily in protest as someone picked their way towards her. Tentatively, Tilly turned in the direction of the sound.

'Jeez, what are you doing?' Monica was carefully picking her way through the debris, followed closely by Maria. Tilly felt her heart squeeze. Why were they there? Had they happened upon her by chance?

'Ugh, God, this thing is a death trap,' Monica exclaimed as she pushed back a strand of hair. She was wearing tight jeans and a grey bomber jacket. Behind her, Maria was also in jeans but in a thick green sweater. Both girls were without their usual mask of makeup.

'What are you–' Tilly clung tightly to her unicorn for protection. 'What are you doing here?'

'Out for a morning stroll,' Maria scoffed angrily. 'What do you think?'

'We came to get you,' Monica said more softly. She had reached the carriage. She carefully rested her long frame against a fallen horse.

'What?' Tilly squinted at her sister in confusion. 'How did you know I'd be here?'

'You're more than a little bit predictable,' Maria noted as she dared to hoist herself onto one of the horses. The pole which attached it to the roof groaned in warning but Maria ignored it as she straddled the horse. If it wasn't for the rust and missing ears it appeared in an almost fit enough condition to ride.

'Predictable?' Tilly repeated.

'We knew you'd be here,' Monica explained coolly, her voice surprisingly level. Tilly had expected her sisters to shout at her, the way they did at one another when they were in the heat of an argument.

'How?'

'You used to love this place,' Maria said as she mockingly kicked the sides of her horse. The carousel gave a disapproving groan.

'Yeah, you always felt safe here. We figured it was where you'd go,' Monica added.

'What happened?' Tilly asked, looking between her sisters. 'This morning when I wasn't there, what happened?'

'Well, Dad was the one who found you gone,' Monica explained, sending a concerned glance in Maria's direction.

'He told us he'd shouted at you,' Maria noted sadly. 'He's sorry.'

'We figured you were upset and gone somewhere to hide. And here you are.' Monica gestured towards Tilly and gave her a pitying smile.

'Why aren't you mad at me?' Tilly inquired. 'Shouldn't you be screaming at me, telling me I should be more responsible? Aren't Mum and Dad mad at me? How come you're being OK about this?'

Monica took a deep breath and looked towards Maria.

'Dad sent us to talk to you,' Maria noted.

Tilly realised how her sisters had comfortably placed themselves within the carousel. They weren't fiercely forcing Tilly from her carriage and marching her home. They were expecting to be there a while. They had come there with more in mind than just bringing Tilly back.

'Talk about what?'

'We know school has been tough on you,' Monica said apologetically. 'And maybe we've not done a great job of helping you out.'

Tilly felt her lips quiver. But she wouldn't cry. She thought of her encounter with Maria, of how mean her sisters had been to her at school. But that was just how sisters were, wasn't it?

'Yeah, squirt, we should have been nicer to you.' Maria admitted.

'What?' Tilly's gaze darted between the pair of them. They were so rarely kind that when they were it instantly made her suspicious.

'Tilly, come on. We're trying to say we're sorry.' Monica stood and came over to the carriage. Tilly braced herself to be hoisted out, but instead Monica elegantly perched upon its edge. She was so close that Tilly could smell her sweet cherry perfume.

Bare-faced and bathed in morning sunlight, Monica looked beautiful. Her sculpted cheekbones and deep-set eyes made her look every inch a princess. Tilly shrivelled beside her.

'But why are you sorry?' Tilly wondered meekly. 'You guys do horrible stuff to me all the time and you've never apologised before.'

'Tilly, there's things you don't know.' Maria said, her voice pained.

'Like what?' Tilly gazed up at Monica, who reached for her shoulder and gave it a squeeze.

'Tilly, we need to talk to you.'

'What's going on?' Tilly demanded. Nothing was making sense. Lack of sleep was making her more irritable than usual. She just wanted to get the shouting part over with so she could go home, take a bath, and go back to bed.

'Tills.' Monica's hand tightened on her shoulder. 'You've no idea what's going on at home, do you?'

'Did you leave because Dad shouted at you?' Maria piped up.

'Yes,' Tilly admitted with a brisk nod. 'He ... he wasn't himself. I just went to check in on him because he was crying in the bathroom and he ...' Till pressed herself against her unicorn. She didn't want to relieve the unpleasant encounter.

'He lashed out,' Monica said sympathetically. 'He's been doing that a lot lately.'

'He has?'

'You really do live in your own little world, don't you?' Maria declared.

'That's not helping,' Monica snapped.

'Sorry.'

'Monica, what's going on?' Tilly pleaded.

'OK.' Monica lifted a hand to stroke Tilly's head. 'I need you to brave and remember that everything is going to be OK. No matter what, Maria and I are here for you. OK?'

'What's going on?' Tilly repeated, her heart conducting a maddening dance of desperation.

Though the sky was clear, Tilly felt storm clouds gathering over her world. She sensed that whatever her sister was about to tell her would change everything.

'Tilly.' Monica inhaled and levelled her gaze upon her little sister. 'Mum is sick.'

'Sick?' Tilly frowned. 'Like she has a cold?'

Behind them, Maria leaned against her carousel horse and titled her head towards the cracked mirrors as though she could no longer face her sisters.

'No,' Monica released a tense breath. 'Not like a cold.'

'Like a stomach bug?'

'No.'

'The flu?'

'No,' Monica pulled her lips into a tight line and shook her head.

'She's the kind of sick where you don't get better,' Maria snapped, still turned away.

'What?' Tilly looked desperately at Monica. 'What does she mean?'

'Oh, jeez.' Monica slid down inside the carriage so she was sat beside Tilly. She drew an arm around her shoulders and pulled her close to her.

'Tilly, have you heard people talk about cancer before?'

Tilly nodded. Cancer was a word people whispered in hushed tones. It was the sort of tragedy that happened to people on TV.

'Well, Mum has that. And it's the bad kind, the kind where she can't get better.'

Tilly heard the words but they refused to sink in. What Monica was saying was impossible. Of course Mum would get better. She had to.

'But Mum will get better though, right?'

'Urgh.' Maria groaned and climbed off her horse. 'I told you she wouldn't get it.' She began wandering towards the back, picking her way across the ride. Her head bowed as she walked away and Tilly thought she heard the whimper of a stifled cry.

'Tilly, I know you like to think the world is like a fairy tale, that we get our happy endings.' Monica rubbed her shoulder as she hugged her tightly. 'But we need you to grow up so you can face this. Mum needs you to be strong and we're worried that you won't be able to handle what she's going through.'

'Mum will get better,' Tilly cried.

'No, Tilly, she won't.' Monica's voice was

firm yet still soft, but there was also a roughness to it, as though it were about to break.

'What does that mean?'

Monica leaned against her little sister, glancing longingly in the direction Maria had disappeared to.

'Monica, what does that mean?' Tilly's voice was fragile.

'It means Mum is going to die.' There was no way Monica could sugar coat the truth, no matter how much she might want to.

'What?' Tilly started to shake.

'Tilly, I know this is hard to accept but me and –'

'When?' Tilly pushed away from her sister and clamoured out of the carriage even though her legs felt unsteady.

'Soon.' Monica lowered her head as her tears fell and splashed against Tilly's shoulders

Tilly wanted to run. She wanted to sprint out of the park and in whichever direction the wind blew her in. She didn't want to stay there as the enormity of what her sister said exploded inside her like a grenade.

First her knees buckled as she dropped to the ground. Then the tears came. Monica was swiftly by her side, clutching her tightly and pressing her against her chest as she wept.

'No!' Tilly wailed. It was the only sound she seemed capable of making. 'No!'

'Shhh,' Monica whispered, her own cheeks streaked with tears. 'It'll all be all right. We will all be okay' but she no longer sounded convinced of her own words. She sounded scared.

Tilly barely remembered the journey home. It was a fog of tears and hysterics. She could vaguely recall being passed between her sisters as they struggled to carry her home. Tilly was unable to walk. Each time they placed her on her own two feet she crumpled like a used tissue.

Eventually they made it back to their house. Thomas was washing himself on the kitchen roof and paused from licking his paw to glance up at Tilly. She stopped crying long enough to look at him. Perhaps it was a trick of her imagination but she could have sworn he looked relieved to see her.

'You found her?' Monica carefully placed Tilly on the stairs as their father entered the hallway.

'Yeah,' Maria stepped in after her sisters and dropped down Tilly's pink backpack. 'She was on the carousel.'

In her despair, Tilly had almost forgotten about her argument with her father. But now she was near him, the memory burned bright and fearful in her mind. Whimpering she turned to climb up the stairs.

'Tilly.' His deep voice stopped her in her tracks. Monica and Maria were beside him, lingering like they weren't sure what to do.

'Tilly, I'm sorry about last night.' He manoeuvred his lean frame so that he was sat beside her on the stairs. He fished in his pocket and pulled out a relatively clean handkerchief which he passed to her. Tilly gratefully swept it across her damp eyes. 'Your sisters explained about what's going on with your mum?'

Tilly nodded numbly.

'It's taken its toll on us all and I'm sorry. OK?' Clive leaned down and kissed Tilly's forehead.

It was a small gesture but suddenly he was her dad again, not some fire-breathing dragon. He was back to being the guy who could fix any broken toy or catch any unwanted spider.

'I can't believe you slept outside all night.' He almost laughed in admiration. 'You've certainly inherited your mother's stubborn streak.'

Tilly dared to glance upstairs.

'She's sleeping,' her dad explained gently. 'But she'll be up in a bit and you can see her then.'

'OK,' Tilly mumbled as she pressed the handkerchief to her eyes to catch more tears.

'You must be frozen.' Her dad pressed the palm of his hand against her head. It was comfortingly warm to the touch. 'Can one of you make sure Tilly has a bath and gets to bed?'

'Sure,' Monica nodded. 'I'll sort her out.'

'Thanks, sweetheart.'

There was no battle at sea, only the vast, endless waves which rolled against the rocks. Tilly wanted a storm. She wanted to splash and send her ships sinking to their watery graves. But a storm required power and energy and she felt drained. Her eyes felt raw and her throat was sore from sobbing but the warm water felt good against her sore limbs. Tilly tried to focus on how everything felt – how her head throbbed, how her muscles ached. It was easier to think of those pains than the one developing in her heart.

Inside, she felt as battered and broken as the carousel. A crack had formed on her heart as deep and wide as any canyon. Tilly could feel it each time she took a breath.

'Tilly.' Monica was knocking against the door. 'You almost done?'

It was the third time she'd asked.

'Five more minutes,' Tilly shouted back. She knew she'd been a while; her skin was already starting to resemble a pack of prunes. But she didn't want to get out. If she got out she'd have to face everyone, including her mother. Tilly had no idea what she was going to say. How do you get someone to stay when they're already in the process of leaving?

Tilly pulled out the plug and sat and watched the bubble-filled water swirl as it departed from the tub. She sat crossed legged, gazing at the end until all of the water had been drained away. Without the warmth, her skin started to prickle. Reluctantly, she stepped out and wrapped herself in a giant, fluffy towel, biting back tears.

That used to be her mother's job – to be standing by the side of a bath with a towel that

Tilly could dissolve into.

'Right, I'm coming in, you'd better be decent,' Monica declared before opening the door. She stepped in as the last of the steam filtered out through the half open window. She was clutching Tilly's nightdress, which she tossed over to her.

'Put this on. You'll probably need to go back to bed for a bit.'

Tilly caught the garment and looked at it blankly. How was she supposed to sleep again? Sleeping was part of normality and Tilly knew her life would never be normal again.

'Put it on,' Monica urged.

Tilly pulled it over her head and let the towel gathered around her drop to the floor.

'How long have you known?' she asked as her head popped out of the top, her cheeks slightly flushed from her bath.

'Since before school started,' Monica replied, folding her arms and leaning against the door frame.

Tilly managed to suppress a sob, making a spluttering sound instead.

'It's a lot to take in.' Monica came over and hugged her. It was such a rare thing for her to do that Tilly almost didn't know how to react. Then her hands connected behind her sister and they were embracing and it felt good. For one brief, blissful moment Tilly felt safe.

'We wanted to tell you sooner.' Monica stepped back, the sadness on her face making her look considerably older. 'Mum and Dad were worried how you'd take it. They ... I don't know,' she sighed. 'They think you might struggle to cope. You're going to have to grow up a lot in a very short amount of time. Can you do that, squirt?'

Tilly was almost glad to hear her sister use the nickname they'd enforced on her. It made the conversation feel more normal.

'I don't know.' Tilly was picking at her fingernails. 'I mean, how am I supposed to do this? How is the world able to keep going?'

Monica reached forward and squeezed Tilly's shoulders. 'I know. It's like our world has been set on fire but everyone else is carrying on like it's a beautiful summer's day. It's pretty messed up.'

Tilly swallowed hard. 'Is she ... in pain?'

'All the time,' Monica replied grimly. 'I guess it's why she sleeps so much. But you'd never know. She's the strongest person in the world. That's why we need to be strong too, to make her proud.'

Tilly didn't think she could be strong. She'd never felt so weak in her entire life. Even breathing was an effort – she felt like she had to remind her body how to do it.

'I'm here for you, OK?' Monica lifted her hands to ruffle Tilly's hair. 'Me and Maria are here for you. We're going through this together. Don't forget that.'

Tilly nodded, squeezing her eyes closed to force back fresh tears.

On the landing, a door creaked. Monica instantly spun around, her eyes wide and alert.

'Looks like Mum is getting up,' she whispered, lowering a protective hand to Tilly's shoulder. 'Do you feel up to talking to her?'

'Yes.' Tilly wanted to run to her mother, wrap herself around her, and never let go. That way she couldn't die, not if Tilly was in the way of death itself.

'Remember, be strong.' Monica squeezed her shoulder once more and let go. Wiping a hand across her eyes, Tilly left the bathroom and wandered towards her parents' bedroom, her bare feet sinking into the carpet. She lifted her chin and pushed back her shoulders so even if she didn't feel it, she at least looked strong.

Wish Upon a Star

'Mum.' Tilly's strong exterior melted away as she fell against her mother. She felt arms wrap around her but they lacked the strength to hold her.

'Come on, Tilly, let's go have a chat.' Her mother drew her into the bedroom where the curtains had been opened, letting in the morning sunlight. 'Do you want to tell me what happened last night?' Ivy asked as she settled on the end of her bed. As the light struck her skin it revealed the tangle of blue veins protruding too close to the surface.

Tilly burrowed her head into her mother's nightdress, which smelt of old perfume and coffee.

'Tilly.' Her mother was gently stroking her

head. 'You did a very silly thing.'

'Mummy.' Tilly was crying. As she hugged her she realised how slight she had become. She could feel the hard line of her ribs beneath the delicate fabric. When had her mother become so slim?

'Please tell me that Monica and Maria are lying, that you're not sick.' Tilly wanted to believe it was a lie. If a fairy were to choose that moment to come down from a star, Tilly would wish for her mother to be well. It was the only thing her heart desired.

'I wish nothing more than to be able to tell you that.' Tilly reluctantly released her grip on her mother so she could look at her. Even though she'd only just got up, she looked tired. Dark circles clung to the bottom of her eyes and her lips were pale to the point of being translucent. If it wasn't for the cracks on them they risked disappearing from sight. 'But Tilly, I'm sick.'

She said the words with pained acceptance.

'You can get better,' Tilly urged.

Ivy sighed and lowered her head. The sunlight which burned against her revealed how thin and brittle her hair had become.

'The doctors have done everything they can.'

Her mother placed Tilly's hands between her own. 'But they found the cancer too late and it's grown too quickly to be contained.'

Tilly stared at her mother's body as if hoping to directly make eye contact with the cancer that was daring to eat her alive.

'They have to make you better,' Tilly told her. 'You can't die, Mummy, you can't.'

'Oh, Tilly.' Ivy was looping an arm around her daughter as she spoke. 'I'm afraid I can. And when I'm gone, I need to know you'll be OK.'

'You can't die!' Tilly cried, the words so loud that her mouth stiffened. 'I won't allow it!' she declared defiantly. 'You can't leave me, Mummy, you can't!'

'I don't want to leave you,' Ivy admitted tearfully.

'Then don't!' Tilly pleaded, her voice shrill. 'The doctors will make you better!'

'Oh, Tilly, my sweet girl. You're going to have to be strong. Can you be strong?'

Tilly shook her head. No, she couldn't. Not when the very ground beneath her feet was giving way.

'Listen to me, Tilly.' Her mother cupped her face with her cold, clammy hands and looked deep into her daughter's eyes. 'I need you to knuckle down at school, you hear me? I need you to focus on being a good student. I won't be here for much longer, Tilly.'

'Why?' Tilly choked on her words. 'Why didn't you tell me?'

Beneath her overwhelming sorrow, the blade of betrayal turned in her back. Her sisters had known for some time but the truth had been hidden from Tilly because she was the baby.

'Because ...' Ivy sighed and released Tilly's cheeks to allow a hand to flutter to her chest. She coughed uneasily for several seconds.

'Mummy?' Tilly was anxiously alert.

'I thought you wouldn't cope,' her mother answered as the coughing subsided. 'You live in a world of fairy tales. I feared what taking that away from you could do.'

'That's why Dad says I need to grow up.'

'Yes.' Ivy spluttered a few more times. 'We need you to grow up, sweetheart, because when I'm gone things will be different.'

Tilly glanced around her parents' bedroom. Her tear-filled eyes made it look like everything was underwater. Everything about the room, about the whole house, was infused with her mother. Ivy's essence was everywhere, from the patterned curtains she'd carefully chosen to the framed pictures of her smiling on her wedding day. If Ivy left there would be no home any more, just a gaping hole where one used to be.

Tilly couldn't help but notice how her mother's nightdress hung on her bony frame. She was already fading away, disappearing before her eyes. How could Tilly have been so blind?

'I can grow up,' Tilly promised as she wiped her eyes. 'I can do better.'

'Oh, sweetheart, it's not about doing better. It's about being able to cope.'

'If I grow up, will you stay?' Tilly bartered.

'It doesn't work like that,' her mother said with a sad smile. 'I've got to leave you no matter how desperately I want to stay.'

'I can't.' Despair bubbled in Tilly's throat. 'Mummy, you can't!' She reached for her mother again and held her with all her might, her hands bunching the flimsy fabric of the nightdress.

'You can't go!' Tilly was sobbing, her body heaving with the effort. 'You're supposed to see me finish school, graduate from university, and get married.'

These things felt light-years away. But

whenever Tilly imagined them her mother was always there. Without her mother in the picture there was no longer a future to imagine at all. The images flittered away like ash in the wind.

'Oh, Tilly.' Ivy was leaning against her daughter, kissing the top of her head. 'I'll be there for all those things, I promise. You won't see me, but I will be there. I'll be with you for the rest of your life.'

'But it's not the same,' Tilly trembled. 'I need you to really be there.'

Tilly had no appetite. Her father placed a freshly-made bacon sandwich down in front of her and eyed her anxiously.

'You must be starving,' he noted. Tilly eyed the slices of white bread and meat and felt her stomach turn unpleasantly. Shaking her head, she pushed the plate away.

'You need to eat,' Clive told her. 'You were out all night. I can't believe you were so foolish, Tilly! You could have caught your death out there!'

He regretted the words the instant he'd uttered them. Clamping a hand to his mouth, he paced towards the kitchen then returned to Tilly's side.

'I didn't mean–'

'It's OK.' Tilly reached for the sandwich with both hands. She felt numb and detached from her movements, as though she were acting a part in a play rather than her own life. 'I'll eat.' She bit down on the sandwich, which would normally be delicious, but today it felt like chewing cardboard – tasteless and dull.

'How was your mother when you left her?'

'Tired,' Tilly told him between mouthfuls. 'She's gone back to bed.'

Her father raked his fingers over the stubble growing on his cheeks.

'I'm going to do better. If it'll help Mum, I'll grow up. I'll work hard in school.'

'Good girl.' Her father smiled gratefully. 'I really am sorry for last night, Tilly. But it is better now you know the truth.'

Tilly wasn't sure. Easier perhaps, but not better. In the space of just a few hours, her entire world had changed. She was no longer a carefree girl who could climb up her bunk bed and escape into a tower – she was turning into someone she didn't recognise and the change was so sudden that she was powerless to fight it.

'You should try and get some sleep,' her father urged. 'You must be exhausted.'

'I'm not tired.' Tilly felt nothing. She was not hungry, nor tired. She was just … empty, as if all her feelings had been absorbed into a vacuum and now she was floating in nothingness. It reminded her of a movie she loved – The Neverending Story. It was about a boy and a magical book and there was even a luck dragon. In the movie the 'nothing' was destroying the magical world. The 'nothing' was just darkness and bit by bit it was devouring Fantasia, the fantasy world in the movie, until hardly anything remained. That was how Tilly felt, as though the 'nothing' was consuming her from the inside out. Only she didn't have a luck dragon or a magical book to rescue her. She just had herself.

'Well, why don't you lie down and try to rest for a while?'

Tilly didn't want to sleep but she didn't want to stay awake either. She was in some sort of weird limbo. Accepting her father's guidance she finished her sandwich, swallowing each mouthful as though it were cement, then climbed the stairs and went to her room.

She had neither the energy nor the inclination to climb up to her tower. Instead, she pushed aside her stuffed toys and lay down beside them. She glanced forlornly at the blank screen of the television at the end of her bed. Normally it had the power to transport her to distant, magical worlds but it couldn't help her now. Nothing could. Tilly was still gazing at the television as her eyes began to close and her breathing began to slow.

A sharp knock on her door caused Tilly's eyes to fly open. As adrenaline pulsed through her body she realised she must have been sleeping. She felt betrayed by her own body – how could it think to sleep at such a time? She pulled herself up as the door opened and her mother walked in. The nightdress was gone and she wore a thick woollen jumper and ill-fitting jeans.

'Sorry, Tilly, did I wake you?' She loitered uneasily in the doorway.

'No,' Tilly insisted, yawning loudly. 'I was up.'

'I've got something for you.' Her mother came in and lowered herself onto the bottom bunk, pain flashing behind her eyes.

'Mum, you should be resting.'

'Here.' Ivy handed her the cardboard box she'd been carrying. Tilly accepted it but didn't pay it any attention.

'Tilly, look,' her mother urged as she nudged her daughter. Inhaling slowly, Tilly looked down at the box. On the front was an image of a sleek, black DVD player. Tilly's eyes widened.

'You bought me a DVD player!' she uttered in disbelief.

'Yes.' Her mother nodded enthusiastically. 'Actually, we bought it in the summer sale and were intending to put it up for Christmas. But I think you could do with it now.'

Tilly gripped the box as her mouth fell open.

'Mum, I don't deserve this.' Hastily, she shoved it towards her mother.

'Tilly, it's fine. It's just a small token but it might help.' Ivy pushed the box back into her daughter's hands.

'Mum.' Tilly didn't know what to say. Her mother had basically given her the magic portal she'd been yearning for. But she didn't want to receive it under these circumstances.

'If I give it back will you get better?'

Ivy shook her head. 'Why don't we set it up together?' she suggested brightly, scooting across the bed and to the small television.

Tilly tilted the box in her hands and scrutinised it.

'Well, open it!'

'OK.' Tilly obliged as she broke the seal and pulled the box open.

An hour later and the DVD player was set up and ready to play one of Tilly's favourite films.

'Will you stay and watch it with me?' Tilly asked hopefully. It would be like old times, the two of them curled up on her bottom bunk. Side by side, they could lose themselves in the magic.

'I can't.' Her mother sighed as she got up, wavering slightly on her feet. 'I need to lie down for a bit. But you watch the movie, sweetheart.'

Tilly wanted to run after her mother as she left the room but she noticed the wilt in her posture. She was heading to bed to rest and all Tilly would do was slow her down.

In spite of the bleakness of the day, the DVD player had provided a glimmer of brightness. Like in the movie about the 'nothing', when the empress' castle is discovered in the endless darkness, shining like an undefeatable beacon of hope.

Excitement fluttered inside Tilly as she thought of the countless hours she could spend watching films. But those feelings were quickly replaced with shame. How could she even consider enjoying herself when Mum was dying? Fresh tears crept from the corners of her eyes.

'So it's true!' Monica barged into Tilly's room and pointed towards the television.

'See, I told you,' Maria declared smugly from behind her.

'What?' Tilly peered out from her bed to look at her sisters. 'What are you doing in here?'

'They gave you a DVD player, jeez,' Monica pouted.

'And no mobiles for us!' Maria pushed her way into the small room to scowl at the television.

'Maybe we should run away,' Monica said.

'Yeah,' Maria agreed with a raise of her eyebrows. 'Maybe then we'd get our bloody phones!'

Monica averted her steely gaze to Tilly, and when she saw her tears some of her anger thawed. She reached for Maria and gave her a quick pinch, nodding in Tilly's direction.

'Reckon you'd let us use the DVD player sometimes?' Monica asked.

'Sure,' Tilly sniffed.

'We could introduce you to some decent films,' Maria added with an overly forced smile.

'You don't have to keep pretending to be nice to me,' Tilly told them. 'You can go back to hating me, it's OK.'

'We don't hate you,' Monica insisted, lowering herself to sit beside Tilly. Maria followed suit and sat on the other side. Wedged between her sisters like bookends, Tilly felt surprisingly content.

'We need to stick together,' Monica told her softly.

'Yeah, squirt.'

'I mean, there are going to be times when we drive each other crazy. We're sisters – that's our job. But we'll always have your back.'

'You can use the DVD player whenever you want,' Tilly told them as they gave her a hug. Huddled together, they truly felt like sisters, a trio of musketeers.

'Thirty minutes, tops!' Her father pointed at her as she sat in front of the computer screen. 'No longer or your eyes will go square!'

Tilly was setting up a Skype call with Josephine. To her surprise, her entire family had been going out of their way to ensure she had a good day. First there was the DVD player, and now time on the computer. Upstairs, her mother was still resting while her father bustled about in the kitchen trying to put together a roast dinner.

Tilly's stomach even managed to growl appreciatively when she smelt the chicken in the oven.

She just hoped Josephine would be online to accept her call. She wasn't sure if she was going to tell her about her mother – she just wanted to see her friend.

After a mere two rings the blue screen faded away and Josephine was there, her smile lighting up the monitor.

'Tilly, hey!' she enthused. Her dark hair was gathered in a neat bun and she wore a lime green jumper which made her seem paler than usual.

'Hi, Josephine.' Tilly couldn't help but smile when she saw her. 'Guess what?'

'What?'

'I got a DVD player in my room!'

'Oh, no way!' Josephine clapped her hands excitedly. Tilly appreciated her friend's enthusiasm, especially when Josephine had all the latest gadgets at her disposal and a huge new bedroom in London with its own bathroom. But she was an only child; she'd never had to endure siblings and sharing like Tilly had.

'And I went out last night,' Tilly added boastfully. Her head lowered slightly. Her parent's anniversary party felt like it had happened a hundred years ago. Had it truly been an anniversary party or something else entirely?

'You did? Where did you go?' Josephine's full attention was focused on Tilly and it felt good.

'Mum and Dad had an anniversary party. It was a lot of fun.'

'Oh yeah, did you dance?'

'Of course!'

Josephine nodded in approval.

'I danced all night!' She even had two sore feet to prove it.

'I'm glad you had fun, Tilly.'

'What did you do?'

'I had a sleepover.' Josephine smiled though there was a guilt-ridden edge to her voice. Sleepovers were something she and Tilly did together. They'd eat big bowls of popcorn and curl up in front of the television.

'That sounds ... awesome.' Tilly managed to smile brightly in response. 'With some of the girls from school?'

'Yeah, a bunch of us. We watched horror movies and painted our nails and ...' Tilly began to zone out as her friend eagerly listed her fun activities. The distance between them started to open up once more even though they were face to face.

'Tilly?'

'Yeah?' Tilly blinked, suddenly brought back to the moment.

'You should come down to London, there's more than enough room. We've got a spare bedroom and everything!'

Tilly felt longing tug at her heart. She'd love nothing more than to escape to London and be with her best friend. She could leave her troubles back in Dullerton. In London, it would be easier to pretend that everything was fine, that her mother wasn't sick.

'I wish I could,' Tilly admitted. Even though Josephine was more polished and preened than before, she was still Tilly's best friend and Tilly was desperate to cling on to the people she had left.

'Tilly, what's wrong?' Josephine noticed the slump in her friend's shoulders and the expression on her face.

Taking a deep breath, Tilly chose to unburden herself.

'My mum is sick,' she admitted.

'Oh, that sucks,' Josephine empathised.

'She's dying.'

The rest of their Skype call involved copious amounts of tears and promises from both girls. The dark cloud which had settled over Tilly's home had managed to reunite them. They reaffirmed their status to one another and when Tilly ended the call, red-eyed and weary, she was certain that no matter what, Josephine would be by her side.

'So how was Josephine?' Her father cautiously peered round the door when Tilly had grown silent.

'She was good.' Tilly wiped at her nose with the back of her hand.

'You told her about Mum?'

'Uh-huh.'

'When things are more settled I promise I'll send you to London. How does that sound?'

Tilly could only nod. By more settled, did he mean when her mother was gone? Thinking about it made Tilly feel like she was teetering on the edge of an immense cliff.

'Did you like the DVD player?' her dad asked, his tone brightening, determined to keep the conversation pleasant.

'Yes,' Tilly uttered. 'Very much.'

'It was Mum's idea,' her father said softly. 'She loves you a lot, Tilly. We both do.'

'Dad! Is dinner ready yet?' Monica stormed into the kitchen, her eyes scanning the sides for signs of a meal being prepared.

'Almost,' Clive sighed, 'give me chance, Monica.'

' I'm starving!' Monica moaned.

'Me too!' a voice chirped from behind as Maria, her sister's ever present shadow, stepped into view.

'We're growing girls, Dad,' Monica told her father.

'All the rubbish you two put away, the only

way you'll be growing is out, not up!' Clive replied.

Monica rolled her eyes and went to inspect the boiling pots on the stove. Tilly had to admire her sisters' resilience. In the face of such tragedy they were both standing tall. Her sisters weren't teenage girls – they were warriors.

Tilly knew she'd never be as strong as them. Early on, she'd realised how set apart she was from Monica and Maria. They were confident and outgoing, she was shy and reclusive. They were tall, she was short. She was the complete antithesis to their dark hair and beauty – at least that's how she felt.

With a full belly, Tilly curled up on the bottom of her bunk bed, feeling oddly content. Her eyes burned from the tears she had shed. During dinner, her mother had made an appearance and tentatively picked at the food on her plate. Tilly told herself that it was a sign, that her mother was getting better.

Leaning against her stuffed toys, Tilly watched one of her DVDs as the sky darkened and night crept in, pushing the sunshine of the day away. In the film, a mermaid dreamed of walking on land and finding love with the prince she'd saved in a storm. She needed a miracle to be with him, and she got one.

Feeling drowsy, Tilly sung along to her favourite songs. She laughed, and stiffened at tense moments. But the mermaid got her miracle. The finale ended with rainbows and promises of a happy ever after.

Slowly, Tilly crept up the ladder of her bunk bed, wanting to be in her tower. As she slumped against the pillows she thought of her Kingdom, and how a decree would be sent out across the lands that the king was in need of a miracle to cure his beloved queen. All the witches, fairies, and magicians would come together to formulate a spell that could overcome any ailment. On rapid wings they'd fly to Tilly's tower to give her the remedy. Tilly's mother would be saved and the kingdom would celebrate with fireworks; because in fairy tales things always seemed dire right before the happy ending.

As Tilly began to drift off to sleep, she thought of a poster hung in the drama room at her school. It had the picture of a rising sun and said 'It's always darkest before the dawn.' Tilly held on to that as she fell asleep.

Off to Work I Go

'It's important to find a book that inspires you.' Mr Hendrix was pacing back and forth in front of his English Literature class, enthusiastically gesturing with his hands. 'You need to find a book that speaks to you.'

Tilly was sat at the back of the room, wedged between Donna Thompson and James Henderson. She was doing her best to focus on what Mr Hendrix was saying but her gaze kept drifting to the large window spread across the entire classroom wall. Tiny droplets of rain were splashing against it as outside it grew so dark that the school's interior lights had to be turned on.

It had been over three weeks since her night spent on the carousel. Three weeks since the ground had collapsed and left her free falling into oblivion. At school it was surprisingly easy to pretend that everything was OK. When Tilly put her head down in class, people assumed she was focused on her work. When she drifted around on her own during break times it wasn't viewed as out of the ordinary. To the outside world, Tilly was just a lonely student trying to survive.

It was less easy to pretend when Tilly was at home. Her house felt like it was made of glass and liable to shatter at any given moment if someone were to say the wrong thing. Monica and Maria had started to go out more. They'd catch buses to the town centre and creep in after dark. Their dad didn't seem to have the energy to punish them. Whenever he wasn't working he sat alone in the front room nursing a large glass of whiskey while his wife slept upstairs. Lately, all Tilly's mother seemed to do was sleep – that and go to hospital. Now that Tilly knew what was going on she was privy to all sorts of information.

'You'll have to let yourself in after school,' her dad had told her over breakfast. 'Your sisters will be out God knows where and I need to take your mum to the hospital. Do you have a key?'

'Yes,' Tilly nodded.

'Good.' Her dad cleared his throat and turned the page of his newspaper even though he wasn't reading it.

'I'll leave you some leftover lasagne in the fridge. Will you be OK to heat it in the microwave?'

There was more nodding on Tilly's part. This was becoming a familiar part of the routine – cooking and eating dinner alone. Tilly had quickly learnt how to use the microwave, something she'd previously thought she was years away from doing.

It would be dark by the time her parents returned, her mother so exhausted that she'd head straight up to bed. Whatever they were doing to her at the hospital only seemed to be making her worse.

'Your homework for tonight is to find something great to read, bring it in tomorrow, and talk about what drew you to it.' Mr Hendrix had his back to the class as he wrote their assignment on the white board.

Tilly reluctantly jotted down the task in her

planner. Homework seemed pointless, as did school. She was trying to participate, to do well, just to make her mother happy but her sense of apathy was increasing.

'I'm going to bring in Little Women,' Donna whispered to Tilly. It was an attempt at forging a tentative friendship between the two of them, but Tilly was too distracted to realise. She just nodded absently.

'Cool.'

'I'm going to bring in Lord of the Flies,' James told the girls before adding boastfully, 'I read it while I was in junior school. What book are you going to bring in, Tilly?'

'I don't know.' The bell was ringing and Tilly was already standing up and shouldering her backpack. There was little she knew anymore. She felt like Alice after she'd tumbled down the rabbit hole. She was in a world where everything was topsy-turvy – where parents could die and children had to make their own dinners.

Tilly opened her lunch box to find that she was yet again without a sandwich. Instead, there was a packet of crisps and two chocolate bars.

Disappointment pulled her towards the polished floor of the food hall like an anchor.

'Hey, squirt.'

Her spirits lifted as Monica slid in across the table. Her dark hair was pulled into a long ponytail and her usual eyeliner was matched with a deep shade of purple lipstick.

'Hey.' Tilly pushed her lunchbox towards her sister. 'Dad forgot to make me a sandwich again.'

'Really?' Monica scrunched up her face in annoyance. 'Remind me tomorrow and I'll rustle something up for you.'

'Are you and Maria going to be home late again?'

'Probably,' Monica shrugged. 'We're meeting some people in the park after school.'

'To do what?'

'Never you mind.'

Tilly leaned forward to retrieve her lunchbox.

'Look, I know things suck at the moment,' Monica said, titling her head. 'And maybe Maria and I should be there more. It's just ...' Her voice trailed off as a group of top year boys walked past. One of them let his gaze linger on Monica for a little too long.

'Can't you come home a little bit earlier?' Tilly pleaded. 'I feel like I'm … alone all the time.'

'Sure.' Monica pulled her purple lips into a kind smile. 'I'll come home earlier in the future, OK?'

Tilly nodded as she opened her packet of crisps.

'Things will get better, Tilly.' Monica reached across the table to give her hand a brief squeeze.

'Will they?' Tilly countered. 'Because I kind of feel things are just going to get worse.'

After lunch came the dreaded double P.E session. Icy trepidation settled in Tilly's stomach as she made her way to the girls' changing rooms. When she walked in, the room was already alive with the incessant chatter of gossip. It smelt of stale sweat and old perfume, which made for an unpleasant combination.

Tilly quietly made her way to the back of the room as she always did and placed her backpack on a hook and found an empty locker.

Though the rain had let up it was still crisp outside. Tilly shivered beneath the thin fabric of her regulation green jogging bottoms. Her teacher was loudly drilling the class about how they'd be running laps around the playing field. In her fleece coat, it must be easy to consider spending the last few hours of the school day in that way. But Tilly, already shaking like a leaf, couldn't think of anything worse. She had hoped the rain would force their class indoors. Maybe they'd play softball or work the gymnastics equipment. Instead, they'd be running around in the cold for two hours.

'She couldn't have picked a better day for it,' Kate mumbled angrily to her minions who were stood beside her, shivering like Tilly was.

'I want at least six laps from everyone!' the teacher declared. Tilly would more willingly donate blood than run round the damp field half a dozen times but she had no choice. With a blow of a whistle, the girls were called to action. The more eager members of the class sprinted ahead, not caring how slippery the grass was. They were just desperate to show off their athletic prowess.

Tilly jogged along with the stragglers at the back. She didn't care if she hit the required six laps or not – she just wanted the time to pass as quickly as possible so she could get back in the warmth.

Even Kate, Sophie, and Claire hung near the back out of a desire not to exert themselves. Tilly had previously overheard Kate in the changing rooms insisting that only losers sweat.

The dark clouds hanging above the field threatened to release more rain. Tilly quietly began to jog around the edge of the playing field and water splashed up the back of her legs from the damp grass. She tried to just focus on what she was doing but without any mental stimulus, her mind started to wander.

She was no longer in her school playing field but out on the open plains of her kingdom. A fierce wind whipped through her hair, carrying with it the promise of an imminent storm. People around her were hurriedly running towards the town to find shelter. Tilly could see it looming on the horizon. Swirling dark clouds gathered together as lightning sparked inside them. When the storm arrived, it would be strong enough to make the strongest buildings shake.

Tilly became afraid. She didn't want to be out in the open when those clouds tumbled in. Some of the villagers noticed she was there and began shouting at her to seek shelter.

'A storm is coming, your Highness!' they cried fearfully. 'You must get back inside!'

More wind tugged at Tilly's long hair. The skirt she was wearing began to billow around her.

'Please, your Majesty,' someone else pleaded, 'you must get back to the tower.'

Tilly nodded, grateful for their concern. She turned and began running, powering her legs beneath her as she broke into a sprint. Distantly, she heard people shouting her name but she kept running and didn't stop until she was safe inside, away from the imminent fury of the storm.

Gasping, Tilly rested her hands on her knees and lowered her head, breathing heavily. Blood pumped furiously in her ears, sounding like distant war drums heralding the start of something awful.

Eventually she straightened and looked around. Gone was the elegant dress she was wearing. Instead, she was in green jogging bottoms and a white polo shirt. Tilly was back in the changing rooms, which were worryingly empty. Where was everyone else?

'Matilda Johnson!' Her P.E teacher pushed

open the doors from outside and powered into the room. 'Young lady, what on earth do you think you are doing?' The robust woman pointed her clipboard in Tilly's direction.

'I …' Tilly gazed helplessly at her teacher. How could she explain that she had been caught up in one of her daydreams without looking mad?

'I've no choice but to give you a detention.' The teacher was forcefully uncapping a pen, her hard gaze remaining on Tilly who was once again shivering.

'I didn't mean to run off,' Tilly admitted.

'Yeah, well, you can think about that in detention.'

Deflated, Tilly handed over her school planner so the detention could be noted down. To add to her humiliation, the rest of her class had started to filter back in as it was almost home time. Tilly tried to ignore their stares and whispered comments.

'You really need to get yourself together,' Tilly's teacher advised as she handed her back her planner. 'You're not in junior school anymore, Matilda. It's time you grew up.'

That was it. Tilly felt something snap inside

her. She threw down her school planner and grabbed her backpack from its nearby hook. She stormed past her teacher and no amount of shouting made her turn back. Still in her joggers and polo shirt, she walked out of the changing rooms, across the tarmacked yard, and out of the main school gates. She didn't stop walking until she was unlocking her front door and stepping into her house.

Monica didn't make good on her word to come home early. Tilly was forced to eat her warmed up dinner alone in front of the television and it was dark by the time everyone came back.

Troubled by the day's events, Tilly did her best to avoid her family. She tucked herself into her lower bunk and put on a DVD. It was a film about a lion cub who thought he'd done something truly awful, so he ran away from his home and everything he knew. Tilly envied his ability to leave. She felt like every part of her life was frayed at the edges.

Eventually, the cub grew up and went back to reclaim what was his but even the light-hearted songs couldn't draw Tilly out of her bad mood.

She turned the film off before it finished. She was tired of hearing the message about how important it was to grow up. Why did it matter so much? Blinking away tears, she began to climb to her top bunk, needing the comfort of her tower.

What was so bad about remaining young? Tilly wasn't trying to hurt anyone by trying to exist within her imagination yet everyone got mad at her when she did.

Tilly was lying in bed when her bedroom door flew open, letting in a square of yellow light.

'Oh my god, squirt!' Maria came bouncing into the room. She smelt faintly of cigarettes underneath the powerful mint scent which coated her words. 'I heard what you did in P.E!'

Tilly rolled over to face her sister.

'You heard?'

'The whole school heard!' Maria enthused, her eyes wide. 'You little rebel! I've never been more proud!'

'Hey, leave her alone.' Monica came in and looked at Tilly. 'What happened today?' There was a kindness in her voice which plucked Tilly's heartstrings in a painful way. She sounded like their mother. Tilly wasn't ready for

Monica to replace their mother.

'Go away,' she told her sister.

'Tilly, you're a certified bad ass!' Maria declared.

'Seriously?' Monica spun around to give her sibling a look. 'You're not helping, Maria.'

'Whatever,' Maria shrugged. 'You should be pleased. After all, now Tilly gets to join the lost cause tribe.'

'I'm not a lost cause!' Tilly objected.

'Sure you're not,' Maria laughed. 'We're all model students in this house, aren't we?' She nudged Monica in the ribs.

'Out.' Monica pointed at the door and with a reluctant sigh, Maria left.

'Tilly, what were you playing at today? You could get in serious trouble.'

Tilly pouted and avoided her sister's gaze.

'Like, are you lashing out because you're angry about Mum?'

'What? No!'

'Then what is it?'

Tilly opened her mouth to speak then snapped it shut. There was no way to explain what had happened in a way that would make her sister understand. It was better for everyone to just think that Tilly was acting out.

'I thought so.' Monica gripped the ladder of the bunk bed so she could lift herself up a few inches and look directly at Tilly.

'We won't tell Mum and Dad,' she offered. 'But you need to sort this out. You can't keep flipping out at school.'

'I didn't –' Tilly wanted to defend her honour but her rebuttal died on her lips.

'I think we're all unravelling one way or another,' Monica said quietly. 'And that's OK. Just make sure that no matter how much you fall apart, you're able to pull yourself back together in the end.'

She dropped to the ground and paused, keeping her eyes focused on her sister.

'You can go,' Tilly told her.

'Are you sure you're all right?'

'No,' Tilly admitted. 'Are you?'

Monica gave a bitter laugh. 'No. I don't think any of us are.'

And with that she left, closing the door behind her.

That morning when Tilly woke, she felt a brick wall of worries tumble against her, flattening her completely and preventing her from getting up.

In that peaceful moment between dreams and waking Tilly was content. The visions which had danced in her mind still lingered and she took comfort in them. But as the fog of sleep was pushed away by the light filtering in beneath her curtains, Tilly was brought back to reality and reminded of everything that was wrong.

Her mother was sick and everyone at school thought she was crazy. These problems wrapped around her lungs and tried to prevent her from breathing. Tilly knew what awaited her when she got out of bed: she'd be eating breakfast alone as her father struggled to stay awake in the kitchen where he was consuming worrying amounts of coffee.

After walking to school she'd have to face her classmates. Everyone would be talking about what she'd done in P.E, pointing and whispering. Tilly's cheeks already burned at the thought of it. If only she could Skype with Josephine before school, but she knew that was impossible. There just wasn't time. Dragging herself out of bed,

Tilly put on her bravest face, counting how many hours it would be until she could escape to her tower.

Tilly had managed to hold her head high as she walked to school despite the incessant whispers which dogged her every step.

'Sticks and stones,' her mother would say. Words couldn't cause physical damage but if you could open someone up and see the wounds on their soul, Tilly was confident they'd be deeper than anything a stick or stone could inflict.

'Oh look, it's Dullerton's newest badass.' Kate smirked as Tilly sat down for registration.

'And here was me thinking you were boring.'

Tilly dropped her backpack underneath her desk and rested her head in her hands. She was in no mood to be teased by Kate.

'You just threw your planner down like you didn't care and stormed out!' Kate continued.

'You impressed me, Tilly.'

Tilly turned her head. Kate normally called her Matilda. Did the use of her nickname mean they were now friends?

'Hey, can you go and check if Daniel is here

yet?' Kate turned to face her friends on her other side.

'He's always late.' Sophie rolled her eyes and frowned.

'Yeah,' Kate agreed with false perkiness. 'But why don't you check for me, OK?'

'Stalk your crushes yourself,' Sophie muttered, but she still got up with Claire and slunk out of the classroom. There was still five minutes before the final morning bell would ring and Miss Havishorn had yet to materialise.

Kate spun around to face Tilly, her bright blonde hair sweeping across her shoulders. 'My dad told me about your mum.'

Tilly flinched. She had anticipated that people would be keen to talk about her antics in P.E, but not about her mother. That was too raw to be up for discussion.

'It sucks, truly,' Kate offered with kindness. 'My mum died when I was six. Car wreck. I've got a step-monster now.'

Tilly was speechless. She could only gape at Kate in astonishment.

'I know, right?' Kate shrugged. 'But yeah, I wasn't born a bitch. This messed up world turned me into one. No one else knows,' she said, lowering her voice. 'I'd like to keep it that way. So, yeah, if you ever want to talk or just have someone there when you curl up into a ball and cry so hard you're worried you've broken all your insides, I'm not all bad, you know.'

Tilly couldn't speak.

'I'm not suggesting we become best friends,' Kate insisted. 'You just don't need to be alone, that's all. Losing your mum is one hell of a kick in the teeth.'

'I've not lost her yet.' Tilly coughed as Sophie and Claire sauntered back, hot on the heels of Daniel West, who completely blanked Kate as he walked in.

'Boys!' Kate scoffed in annoyance.

Registration was almost over when Miss Havishorn glanced up from behind her desk and looked towards the back of the room.

'Matilda, can you hang back before your next class, please?' Although it was delivered as a question, Tilly knew it was an order.

'Duh duh duh!' one of the boys at the front of the class remarked, which made those around him giggle.

'Calm down,' Miss Havishorn snapped. The bell tolled and everyone was able to leave, except for Tilly who had to shamefully slink to the front of the room.

'I believe that this is yours.' Miss Havishorn opened up a drawer and retrieved Tilly's school planner, which was significantly more dog-eared than it had been at the start of term.

'Thanks,' Tilly mumbled as she accepted it.

'I was not pleased to hear about yesterday's display, Matilda,' Miss Havishorn explained, pushing her glasses up her nose.

'About that –'

'But you don't need to worry about the detention. I spoke to Miss Grey.'

The P.E. teacher?

'What do you mean?' Tilly asked.

'There's no detention,' Miss Havishorn clarified. 'I explained to Miss Grey about your … situation.'

Tilly blinked.

'What situation?'

Miss Havishorn sighed and clamped her plump hands together.

'Matilda, I know what's happening with your mother. Your father contacted the school.'

Tilly lowered her head in shame. What was happening at home was separate to her life at school and now the two were bleeding together. Did everyone think that she couldn't cope? That she needed to grow up?

'You're going through a tough time,' Miss Havishorn continued. 'It's only natural that you'll feel angry and upset. If you feel it would benefit you to visit the school counsellor then I can arrange that, Matilda, just –'

'Tilly.' She boldly interrupted her teacher mid-sentence.

'Sorry?' Miss Havishorn frowned.

'My name is Tilly. I don't like to be called Matilda.'

Miss Havishorn lifted her eyebrows in surprise.

'Very well, Tilly.' She said the name as though it were an ill fit. 'If you would like to see the counsellor, let me know.'

'Is that it? Can I go now?' Tilly asked as she looked towards the door.

'Yes,' Miss Havishorn nodded. 'But Matil – Tilly, make sure you don't lose yourself. These are formative years. I'd hate to see this tragedy shape you in a negative way.'

'I hardly see how it could shape me positively,' Tilly snapped as she turned and strode out the door. As she was absorbed into the flow of students hurrying down corridors and hallways, she didn't allow herself to be pushed and shoved like a feather caught in an updraft. Tilly locked her jaw and used her elbows to force her own path through the sea of jumpers.

Tale as Old as Time

Rain whipped against Tilly's bedroom window as she sat on her bunk bed, her head down in concentration. Carefully, she manoeuvred the scissors through the piece of coloured paper she'd sneakily brought home from school.

'I don't care!' Monica's angry words travelled across the landing, slightly muffled by Tilly's closed bedroom door. 'I'm getting a ride with Andrew. It's not my problem how you get there!'

Doors were slammed. Heavy footsteps stomped across the landing in the direction of Tilly's room.

'Can you believe her?' Monica asked as she swung the door open.

Tilly ceased cutting and glanced up at her sister. Monica's cheeks were flushed. Her wet hair fell down her back and was starting to curl, as it always did when it was left to dry naturally. Any kinks would be ironed out later with expert precision.

'She's mad because I'm not going with her to the ice rink.' Monica was tapping her left foot, one hand draped against her waist.

'You're going with Andrew,' Tilly said.

'You heard?'

'The whole street heard.'

'Yeah, well,' Monica shrugged. 'Andrew is in college and has a car. Of course I'm going to go with him instead of riding the bus with Maria.'

'I heard that!' a muffled voice snapped from behind a distant door.

'Does Mum know?' Tilly asked innocently.

'Does Mum know what?'

'That you're getting a lift with a college boy.'

The red shade of Monica's cheeks darkened.

'Squirt, do yourself a favour and stop being a goody two-shoes, OK? Mum doesn't know. And it's going to stay that way.'

'She probably heard you shouting.'

'Please, lately she sleeps like the dead.'

As Tilly tensed, the scissors she'd been holding slid from her fingers and dropped to the floor.

'Oh, crap, I'm sorry.' Monica slapped a hand against her temple and came to sit beside Tilly.

'I'm not … I'm just not thinking.' She looped an arm around Tilly's shoulders and pulled her close. 'I'm on my period,' Monica added quietly.

'It's OK.'

Their peaceful moment was rudely interrupted as Tilly's bedroom door was pushed open with such force that it smacked against the wall, causing it to shudder.

'You're giving me a lift!' Maria strode over to the bunk and glowered at her sisters. She looked comical with only half of her hair straightened.

'We always go together, Monica! I don't care how fit this Andrew is!'

'Do you have your period too?' Tilly wondered. They were both being overly irrational.

'Yes!' both girls snapped in unison.

'It's some weird thing, women who live together end up in sync,' Monica explained with a roll of her eyes.

'I'm going to the rink with you,' Maria declared.

'Fine.' Monica threw up her hands in defeat and gracefully departed the lower bunk.

'Good.' Maria hadn't expected such an easy victory. The anger which simmered within her was suddenly without an outlet.

'Come on, I need you to do my hair.' Monica was halfway out of the room, but Maria remained where she was.

'Squirt, what are you doing tonight?'

Tilly had been reaching for her scissors. She froze, hand extended.

'Me?' she asked.

'Yeah, you!' Maria confirmed.

'You're not suggesting she comes with us, are you?' Monica asked from the doorway.

'Well ...' Maria twirled a strand of hair around her finger. 'I was twelve when you first took me to the disco at the rink. Maybe she should come with us.'

Monica pursed her lips together as she considered it.

'What do you think, squirt? You want to come?'

Tilly was stunned. Her sisters had never thought to include her in their plans before. A part of her fluttered with excitement at the prospect of going to the ice rink for the weekly disco. She'd heard stories of what went on there. Hearts were won and broken in the space of one song.

She looked down at the coloured paper she'd carefully been cutting. She wasn't ready to step into her sisters' world yet. Somehow she sensed that once she began donning eyeliner and wearing her hair poker straight there would be no going back, no reclaiming the person she'd once been.

'I've actually got plans,' she told them. 'But thanks for asking.'

'So, next time?' Maria glanced towards Maria, who was already heading back towards their bedroom.

'Yeah,' Tilly smiled. 'Next time.'

Maria started walking after her older sister, but she paused as she reached the landing and turned around.

'What plans do you have tonight?'

'I'm doing something with Mum.'

'Oh,' Maria didn't seem to know how to take it. She nodded then walked off.

'Yeah.' Tilly smiled to herself as she resumed cutting out shapes. 'I've got plans with my mum.'

It was seven o'clock and Tilly had been shut up in her bedroom all day, only emerging to have dinner. Her hands felt stiff from having held the scissors for so long but she was finally happy with the finished product.

'You are not going out like that!' her dad's appalled voice carried from the hallway downstairs.

'Dad, everyone dresses like this!' Monica declared. Tilly crept out of her room and sat on the landing, out of sight from her family gathered below. She used to love sneakily watching people. She found it strangely comforting – as if witnessing drama unfold made her somehow a part of it.

Both Monica and Maria were wearing black miniskirts and tights which seemed to have been deliberately slashed to ribbons.

'You're a state!' Clive insisted, gesturing at their legs. 'You look like vagabonds.'

'One, I don't know what this is.' Monica was listing her points on her fingers, showing off freshly-painted silver nails. 'Two, we look hot!'

This made Maria giggle.

'I can't let you go out like that!' Clive declared, though he gave an exasperated sigh which signalled imminent defeat.

'It's too late anyway, we've got to go else we'll miss the bus.' Monica was opening the front door.

'Yes, the bus,' Maria giggled. Clearly their father wasn't privy to their plans, which involved getting in cars with college boys.

'Be home by eleven!' Clive leaned out of the door and shouted. 'I mean it! Dammit.' He thrust his hands into his trouser pockets and lowered his head.

'Dad?' Tilly stood up and approached the top of the staircase.

'What is it?' Her dad lifted his gaze to look at her. He was still wearing his work clothes which were stained and faded beyond recognition.

'Is Mum still sleeping?'

'Probably,' Clive sighed.

'Can you wake her up?'

'What? Tilly, no.' He removed a hand from his pocket to wave at his daughter. 'You know we need to let her rest.'

'But I've made her a surprise.'

'Tilly, it can wait until tomorrow.'

'No, it can't.'

Clive pushed a hand through his thinning hair.

'Why can't it wait?' he asked, managing to keep his voice level.

'Because tomorrow isn't an option anymore,' Tilly said. 'Tomorrow Mum might be gone. Tomorrow I might go to the ice rink with Monica and Maria and a part of me will be gone too.'

This made her father nod thoughtfully.

'They asked you to go?' He peered up at her with sad eyes.

'Uh-huh.'

'And you said no?'

'Uh-huh.'

'Good girl,' he complimented, still ruffling a hand through his hair. 'You're not going to be twelve forever, are you?'

'Nope,' Tilly replied with certainty.

'Maybe there's something to be said for not being in a hurry to grow up,' her father said as he began to walk up the stairs. 'All your sisters want to do is cover their faces in make-up and chase boys. I don't know what I'll do with them when –' He stopped himself. 'Let's see if your mum is awake.'

'OK.'

Tilly watched her father quietly approach his bedroom door and ease it open. As he did so, he released the tainted, built-up air. It spilled out on to the landing, pungent with medicinal undertones. Tilly recoiled as she inhaled it. She loathed the smell. It seemed to cling to everything her mother touched, like she was bringing a part of the hospital home with her.

It was a smell Tilly recognised from when she'd gone to visit her grandmother just before she'd died. It was a smell she'd forever associate with death and decay.

'Ivy,' Clive timidly called, and in the darkness something stirred. 'Hey, baby.' He let the air envelope him as he went inside but Tilly remained on the landing. She no longer liked to go into her parents' bedroom. The bedside table was now littered with pill bottles and tissues instead of books and perfume. The curtains were always drawn together, plunging the room into an eternal night time. The putrid smell of sickness tried to creep into Tilly's bones each time she was forced to breathe it in.

A few minutes later, Tilly's mother emerged, bleary-eyed from the darkness, her husband supporting her as she took tentative, pained steps. She was a skeleton underneath the robe she'd hastily pulled on. She looked worn out, like a toy that had been played with too many times.

But when she saw her daughter she smiled, and her smile still warmed her faded features.

'Hi, sweetheart. Your dad says you've made me a surprise.'

'That's right,' Tilly replied. She reached for her mother's hand and held it tightly within her own, and slowly guided her across the small landing. 'I've been working on it all day,' Tilly explained.

'I can't wait to see it.'

'I'll be right downstairs if you need me,' Clive whispered to his wife before kissing her cheek and descending towards the hallway.

'Mum.' Tilly paused at her bedroom door. 'You know how everyone is always telling me I have to grow up?'

'Yes, sweetheart.'

'And I get that I need to,' Tilly nodded, 'but

sometimes all I want to do is live inside all my fairy tales because it's safer there. There's no cancer, only happily ever afters.'

'It's a nice thought, Tilly.'

'But I was thinking that maybe, just for tonight, we could both escape, just for a little while – like we used to do when I was little.'

'I remember,' Ivy smiled.

'We'd curl up and watch movies. We'd watch films about princesses and brave explorers. Mum, you showed me a world where I never had to be scared or alone.'

Ivy swallowed as a solitary tear slid down her pale cheek.

'And I want to take you there with me, just for tonight.' Tilly pushed open her bedroom door and her mother gasped.

Hundreds of paper streamers hung across the ceiling and draped around the bed, transforming the room so it looked like a grotto. Tilly had painstakingly cut out dolls, snowflakes, butterflies – anything she could think of. And now the paper streamers had managed to make her room look like it was magic.

'Oh, Tilly.' Ivy stepped inside, bending to avoid some of the low hanging streamers. A hand fluttered up to her throat. 'It's ... it's beautiful.'

'I was thinking we could watch some of our old movies.' Tilly pointed towards her lower bunk. Gone were the stuffed toys, who were now up in the tower. In their place were all her pillows, as well as both duvets. She'd created a snug nest which her mother could comfortably lie in.

Ivy wiped at her eyes. 'That would be lovely.'

Slowly and carefully, she positioned herself so she was half sitting, half lying down. Tilly turned on the television and grabbed the remote before shuffling in beside her mother. Although she smelt medicinal, Tilly could still make out the faint hint of vanilla which stubbornly clung to her mother's clothes. Tilly smiled as she smelt the sweetness; it reminded her that somewhere beneath the sickness her mother was still there.

'So what are we watching?' Ivy asked.

'Your favourites,' Tilly told her with a smile. 'Starting with Beauty and the Beast.'

'Ah yes.' Ivy nuzzled contentedly against her daughter. 'That was always one of my favourites.'

Tilly was smiling so much that her cheeks

were beginning to ache, but she didn't care. This was all she'd ever wanted – to step into a fairy tale with her mother by her side.

'What time do you call this?'

A door slammed downstairs and Tilly was abruptly woken up. Rubbing her eyes, she sat up and for a moment was confused that she was on her bottom bunk. Then she spotted her mother sleeping soundly beside her and it all came flooding back. The bedroom light was still on, illuminating the streamers in all their glory. On the television, the DVD screensaver had come on. At some point during their third movie both Tilly and her mother had fallen asleep.

'Dad, relax, it's only half eleven!' Monica shouted.

'What time did I tell you to be home?' Clive asked, his voice as sharp and direct as a steel blade.

'Urgh!' Monica exclaimed. Footsteps thundered up the stairs and Tilly turned towards her mother.

'Mum, do you want to stay here or go back to bed?'

Ivy's eyes remained closed.

'Mum?' Tilly reached for her and nudged her shoulder.

'Mum?' Tilly was almost shouting now, nudging her mother so forcefully that she'd surely awaken. But Ivy's eyes remained tightly shut.

'Mum!' Tilly was screaming, the sound erupting out of her like a volcano. Seconds later, her bedroom door was thrown open causing her paper streamers to shudder in the sudden wind.

'What's going on?' Clive demanded, his face devoid of colour.

'It's Mum!' Tilly wailed, clamouring out of her lower bunk. 'She won't wake up!'

Clive was leaning down towards his wife, slapping her cheeks to try and stir her. 'Call 999!' He turned and barked the order to Tilly, but Monica was in the doorway and dashed off.

'Is she going to be all right?' Tilly sobbed, her cheeks quickly becoming waterfalls. 'Why won't she wake up?'

'I don't know!' Clive snapped, his back to her. 'Come on, baby, wake up,' he whispered to his wife. 'Please, I can't do this without you.'

Tilly could only stand by and watch as

paramedics stormed into her room. They didn't pause to notice the paper streamers. They spoke to Tilly's mother in urgent tones, but still she didn't wake. Carefully, they pulled her out from the bed and placed her on a gurney. An oxygen mask was placed over her mouth and nose and someone began fiercely tapping the back of her hand.

'Tilly, come on.' Monica pushed her way into the room to lead Tilly out on to the landing.

'You shouldn't have to see that,' she told her as they went down to the kitchen.

Tilly couldn't speak. She was trembling and crying. Monica and Maria were with her. They were equally silent. They exchanged panicked glances, but said nothing.

After ten long minutes they heard the paramedics carrying their mother down the stairs. They were all holding their breath as the door to the kitchen opened.

'I'm going to the hospital with her,' their dad told them.

'Is she awake?' Tilly spluttered, suddenly finding her voice.

'Look after her,' Clive told his older daughters. 'I'll be home as soon as I can.'

When Tilly opened her eyes, she saw sunlight filtering in through her streamers, casting strange shapes across the floor. Again, her body had betrayed her. After what had probably been the worst night of her life, she had managed to fall asleep. Pushing her hair out of her face, Tilly sat up and looked around. She was on her bottom bunk, wrapped in two duvets and leant against a large pile of cushions. The streamers she had so carefully hung the night before now looked ragged and tattered. Many had fallen in the night or been knocked down by all the people who had tried to squash into her small room.

Tilly choked as she looked at the broken butterflies and snowflakes trampled into the carpet.

Her mother.

Her heart flip-flopped with panic as she scrambled from her bed. Where was she? Was she home? Tilly ran from her room and raced across the landing. She barged into her parents' room, praying that her mother would be there, curled up on her side on the far side of the bed. But even in the darkness Tilly could see that the bed hadn't been slept in, the sheets still neatly made.

Staggering back, Tilly dropped to her knees. Why hadn't her mother come home? Where was her father?

Beside her, a door creaked open and Monica looked out. Dark circles gathered beneath her eyes.

'Tilly, you're up.' Her voice was hoarse as though she'd been using it too much. She came out of her room and dropped down to sit beside Tilly.

'Where's Mum?' Tilly asked, her lip trembling.

'She's at the hospital,' Monica explained as she rubbed a hand up and down her back. 'She was unconscious for a while but they managed to revive her at three in the morning. Dad is still there with her. He's called to say we can go and see her when it's visiting hours.'

Tilly had never been more relieved in her life. She embraced Monica tightly, her tears soaking into the Sons of Cherry T-shirt her sister loved to sleep in.

'I thought she'd died,' Tilly admitted as the terror which had been building up inside her began to ease away.

'We all did,' Monica whispered. 'It was pretty scary.'

'But she's OK, she'll be all right?'

'Yeah,' Monica squeezed her tightly though she still sounded sad, 'she'll be all right.'

Tilly felt uneasy the moment they walked into the hospital. Everywhere she looked there were people being pushed around in wheelchairs or staggering alongside a drip on wheels. Her mother didn't belong here.

The same medicinal smell which inhabited her parents' bedroom coated every corridor, though there was also a pungent smell of stale urine which made Tilly want to vomit. Somehow she remained composed as she followed her sisters towards the ward her mother was in.

Monica turned to look at her. 'Remember what Dad said. Be upbeat, OK? And don't freak out about all the wires and stuff.'

'Wires and stuff?' Tilly was still pondering the thought as they rounded a corner and saw her mother. At least, she saw the parts of her mother which weren't being obscured by the machines now attached to her.

'Hey,' Ivy spoke when they came close but her words were barely audible thanks to the oxygen mask covering her face.

'Here, let's take that off for a bit.' A nearby nurse leaned over to remove the mask and Tilly's mother took in a deep, satisfied breath.

'Are these your daughters?' the nurse asked.

'Yes,' Ivy nodded, her eyes glittering with pride.

'You've got three stunners.' The nurse squeezed Ivy's hand before heading to the end of the next bed to pump antibacterial hand wash and check the patient's chart. Tilly's own hands were still sticky from the clear gloop her sisters had insisted she use when they'd walked in.

Three stunners. Tilly looked at the nurse as if she were mad. Two stunners, yes, but definitely not a third one.

'I'm so pleased to see you,' Ivy cried a little breathlessly.

'Mum, are you OK?' Monica was hugging her while Maria waited her turn.

'We were so worried about you,' Maria whispered.

'I'm sorry I gave you such a scare,' their mother apologised. 'Apparently, my heart is getting a bit sluggish but the doctor says some medication will sort that right out.'

'That's great, Mum.' Monica squeezed Ivy's hand, careful to avoid the needles placed into the back of it.

'Do you girls think you could pick me up some magazines?' Ivy looked between her two oldest daughters. 'I've been so bored just lying here.'

'Sure, Mum.' Monica tugged Maria away from the bed, glancing protectively at Tilly before heading to the main area of the ward.

'How's my little Tilly?' Ivy's words were warm but sounded bittersweet. Tilly cautiously approached the bed. Her mother looked as though she'd been caught in some hideous spider's web thanks to all the plastic wires which gathered around her.

'Was this my fault?' Tilly asked shamefully. She'd been the one to insist her mother partake in her surprise. If only she'd let her rest, maybe none of this would have happened.

'Of course not!' Ivy's eyes widened, appalled. 'I had a lovely time with you.'

'You did?'

'Yes,' Ivy smiled. 'It was lovely to escape into fairy tales for a while.'

Tilly moved further up the bed so she was stood directly beside her mother, who was propped against numerous pillows.

'But Tilly.' Her mother struggled to lift her arm and reach for her. Tilly met her halfway and they held hands.

'Yes?'

'I know how much you love escaping into fairy tales.' Ivy paused to cough and her breath rattled worryingly in her chest. The nurse at the nearby bed paused from checking notes on a patient to cast a wary glance over. 'Tilly.' Her mother cleared her throat and managed to continue. 'You can't stay in a world of make believe, as tempting as it is. You must grow up, sweetheart; especially in the face of what's to come.'

Tilly stiffened and forced herself to smile. Again, everyone was telling her to grow up. But what good did that do? Growing up would surely mean losing her mother? What was wrong with wanting to stay as things were, with refusing to let anything change?

'Will you be coming home soon?' Tilly asked hopefully.

'Yes,' Ivy nodded. 'In a week or so, they reckon.'

'Good.' Tilly didn't like not having her mother home. It made the house feel incomplete, like a jigsaw with an entire portion missing. Without those pieces you couldn't even tell what the main image was meant to be.

'When I come home I want to hear about how well you're doing at school, you understand?'

'Yes, Mum.'

'We got what we could.' Monica and Maria returned with a small stack of magazines which Maria casually tossed onto the end of the bed.

'They had a terrible selection,' she frowned.

'We did our best.'

'Your dad is about somewhere.' Ivy strained in her bed to try and look beyond her small section of the ward. 'Make sure he gets you girls something good for dinner, not just a takeaway.'

'OK,' Monica nodded.

Tilly ate the last of her McDonalds and sipped thoughtfully on her milkshake. Her bedroom had been restored to its normal state. The collection of cuddly toys had resumed their residence on the bottom bunk and the paper streamers were now in the bin, as if the previous night had never happened. But it had. Tilly had yet to realise how she'd carry that night with her for the rest of her life.

Tilly looked at her Happy Meal box. Her sisters had ordered adult meals but Tilly was drawn to the children's option and she didn't even care. Her mother and everyone else were wrong when they told her she had to grow up. Growing up would mean accepting that the world was falling apart.

Beyond the small confines of her room, she heard the distant chants of her townspeople. They were worried for their Queen and for the princess who was at risk of being left alone.

But as Tilly heard their cries carry across the grassy plains towards her town she knew that with them around she'd never be alone. They would always be looking out for her. Emboldened by their presence, Tilly began to climb her tower. She was carefully navigating her way past the thorny rose bushes and shivered against the increasingly cool air.

Panting, she reached the top. Sweeping across her familiar room, she hurried past her grand four-poster bed and went to the opposite window, pushing open the wooden shutters. Brisk air enveloped her as she leaned out, her hands resting on the stone brickwork. From this side of her tower she could just make out the edge of the ocean breaking against a distant shore.

A pale blue sky stretched out, granting her an impressive view of her beloved kingdom. People scurried about below her like ants. Tilly waved down as the wind tugged at her long, loose hair. She was smiling and felt lighter, less burdened by her troubles.

'I'm home!' Tilly bellowed out from her tower, letting her voice carry on the wind across the realm.

'And I'm never going to leave!'

With Special Thanks to

The Accent YA Editor Squad

Aishu Reddy

Alice Brancale

Amani Kabeer-Ali

Anisa Hussain

Barooj Maqsood

Ellie McVay

Grace Morcous

Katie Treharne

Miriam Roberts

Rebecca Freese

Sadie Howorth

Sanaa Morley

Sonali Shetty

With Special Thanks to

The Accent YA Blog Squad

Agnes Lempa

Aislinn O'Connell

Alix Long

Anisah Hussein

Anna Ingall

Annie Starkey

Becky Freese

Becky Morris

Bella Pearce

Beth O'Brien

Caroline Morrison

Charlotte Jones

Charnell Vevers

Claire Gorman

Daniel Wadey

Darren Owens

Emma Hoult

Fi Clark

Heather Lawson

James Briggs

James Williams

Jayana Jain

Jemima Osborne

Joshua A.P

Karen Bultiauw

Katie Lumsden

Katie Treharn

eKieran Lowley

Kirsty Oconner

Laura Metcalfe

Lois Acari

Maisie Allen

Mariam Khan

Philippa Lloyd

Rachel Abbie

Rebecca Parkinson

Savannah Mullings-Johnson

Sofia Matias

Sophie Hawthorn

Toni Davis

Yolande Branch

For more great books, and information
about Carys Jones, go to:

www.accentya.com